HUNTER

For Patti Gauch,
who knew this story came from a deep place and who
journeyed with me, page by page, smoothing the way
with wisdom and skill.

HUNTER

Joy Cowley

PHILOMEL BOOKS

NEW YORK

PATRICIA LEE GAUCH, EDITOR

Published simultaneously in Canada.   Printed in the United States of America.
Designed by Semadar Megged.   Text set in 11-point Sabon.

Library of Congress Cataloging-in-Publication Data
Cowley, Joy.   Hunter / Joy Cowley ; Patricia Lee Gauch, editor.   p. cm.
Summary: A Maori boy in 1805 and a plane crash survivor marooned on a deserted
island in 2005 experience interconnecting visions.   1. Maori (New Zealand people)—
Juvenile fiction. [1. Maori (New Zealand people)—Fiction. 2. Visions—Fiction.
3. Aircraft accidents—Fiction. 4. Survival—Fiction. 5. New Zealand—Fiction.] I.
Gauch, Patricia Lee. II. Title.   PZ7.C8375Hw 2004   [Fic]—dc22   2003012502
ISBN 0-399-24227-9
10 9 8 7 6 5 4 3 2 1
First Impression

J ordan realised that she had been holding her breath. She filled her lungs, easing the ache in her chest. Gliders landed safely all the time, and they didn't have engines. So what if Harold didn't like kids? He was a good pilot. He knew the beach was here. He knew he could land on it. He'd probably landed on it before. Heaps of times.

In the silent approach, they could have talked to each other, but they didn't. There was nothing to say. The red light pulsed like a heartbeat and above it, the yellow beach slowly unwound. They were so close to the sea that at any moment the wheels must break the surface. But it wasn't water they touched. There was a bump and they bounced, up in the air, down again, bump, bump, running fast along crunching stones. Harold had his elbows out, working the controls. Still going fast. The beach was narrow, sea on one side, trees on the other, and they were halfway along it. The plane was slowing, slewing sideways in the gravel. Harold struggled and swore.

Near the end of the beach the left wing caught a tree. What happened then seemed like a film in slow motion. Jordan saw the plane make a deliberate turn and saunter toward a large old beech tree. Branches of the tree came to meet them, scattering leaves, twigs, glass, in a great shower.

The branches entered the cockpit right through to the backseat, and the plane stopped.

1 8 0 5

He was alive because he was a hunter. He had the gift, a way of seeing things that were hidden, the eel under a ledge in a stream, birds nesting in rushes or holes in the ground. If his captors killed him as they had killed other slaves, their storehouses would be leaner. He knew it. They knew it. But the knowing did not prevent them from treating him as one of the dogs.

Hunter bent his head against the rain that came down from the mountain cloud, fast and hard, biting like tattoo needles, although at this time of the year it was not cold. Water ran in small streams over his hair to his chest, to the sodden sealskin at his waist. His feet, too, were wrapped in sealskin roped with flax cords, and although he could move faster with bare feet, the hides protected him from the beach stones that lay as sharp as spearheads to the sky.

The warriors were behind him, Te Hauwai grunting softly as he climbed a rock slippery with seaweed,

Manunui shaking his head to release the rain. Toru was farther back, shouldering the flax kit of baked yam and potato. They were older men carrying large bellies of good living, and neither the weather nor the way gave them satisfaction. It did not please them that they should walk in the footsteps of a slave with no name whose tribe had lost the right to breathe.

Toru's resentment was especially strong. Hunter understood it was difficult for Toru to accept that a despised slave had the gift of Tane, god of the forest. Who knew why he possessed such a gift? How there came to the eye of Hunter's mind the great moa that no one had seen in many generations. He had seen it before in his *moe-mahi*, his waking dreams, a huge flightless bird, twice the height of a man, in a glacier-carved valley between two mountain ranges. He spoke of his vision to the boys in the village and soon everyone knew—moa had not vanished from the earth. At least one of the great birds was still alive.

Usually the three men left hunting to the younger warriors of the tribe, youths the same age as the slave. But this was not an ordinary hunt. It carried much *mana*, much honour.

Not all believed the boy's vision. "It cannot be true," some said. "The moa rests with our ancestors."

But Te Hauwai knew the truth of it. The no-name's seeing came from Tane, and the god of the forest did not lie.

As for Manunui, his forebears had been the greatest of

2

moa hunters, and their skill had been carved into the wood of the *wharenui,* the big meeting house where past and present generations breathed together. Did not Manunui's full name—Manunui-a-te-maunga—mean "Great-bird-of-the-mountain"? Did not Manunui wear the triumphs of his ancestors carved into his face? Whoever looked on the tattoo of Manunui must understand the importance of this chase.

"The dog is lying," said the woman of Manunui, believing her man too old for a long journey into the mountains.

"It is not the boy. The no-name is nothing," he'd replied. "The seeing comes from Tane himself."

Now, a day's journey from the village, in driving rain and over land that had become much rougher and steeper since he last walked on it, Manunui-a-te-maunga was ready to doubt anything, even the voice of Tane. The boy had never been wrong before, but then he had never seen a moa before. Who was to say that the slave had not made up this vision? It could be a trick.

Te Hauwai was holding the same doubts. "If there is no moa at the end of our journey, that maggot will have my spear in his heart, I promise you."

Toru said nothing, but of the three, he was the most dangerous. He could throw an axe with deadly aim and had once killed a man who had laughed at him.

Hunter heard their mutterings and understood their

discomfort. He stopped on the wet stones and dropped onto his haunches, head bowed, indicating that they should rest awhile. The men moved back under a tree and sat on a bed of fern and moss, spears at their sides, their bellies resting on their crossed legs, their shoulders heaving to regain breath.

Hunter knew that if he could get past their throwing arms, he could easily outrun them.

This place, known as the bay of the dying moon, had a small, narrow beach that curved between rocky headlands. In front of Hunter lay the dark water of the sound, ringed with raindrops. On each side, rocks shone like wet seals and the steep mountains, covered with beech and *rimu,* were wrapped in grey mist. All around him was the sound of water: rain on leaves, stones, skin; rain on the flat black sea; and the bigger song of waterfalls that fell from the tops of cliffs, scarcely touching their paths of mosses and ferns.

Keeping his head lowered, Hunter let his eyes move sideways to the valley between two rows of peaks. There were no tracks. The bush was thick, the way would be steep and difficult. If the men suffered, they would find a reason to beat him. His eyes closed as he shrugged away the insect crawl of rain on scarred skin where sticks had opened up old whip marks. How many beatings? He did not know. Slaves and dogs alike were trained with lashes. Another beating was likely. These three men, grown soft from age and good eating, could not travel far. It would have been better for them if they had put aside their pride and sent young warriors for the hunt.

Now the moa seemed to move inside Hunter. He could hear it, smell its odour, sharp and hot. In the seeing of his mind, the wind parted long brown feathers on the moa's breast, showing deep colours of grey and black, and a head almost bare of plumage. The beak was big enough to take a man's hand, but the strongest thing was its eye, sharp with watching and full of yellow light. It walked slowly, with high steps, putting each foot down carefully, flexing its claws.

As it walked, the long neck moved back and forth in even rhythm, stopping only when the moa paused to look at something. Hunter breathed in its smell and knew it must be close. He was sorry that such a rare bird had to be killed, and wished he had not spoken of his vision. It was too late for regret. Now, if the men did not find the bird, he would be severely punished, and he had no parent or older brother to defend him.

Hunter remembered nothing of his family. He was perhaps four summers when they were killed, maybe five. His memory refused to go back that far. He knew only captivity and hunting, and as long as his gift continued, the people would allow him to survive.

He shrugged, hardly aware now of the rain that ran down his back and neck. Indeed, he would survive, but he would not leave that decision to the village. The idea of escape had always been in him. For years it had been a mere seed. Now it swelled with life. The valley of the moa was far from the village and these men were too old for a chase. He could easily leave them behind.

"I will have the skin," Te Hauwai was saying. "Of all the leaders of the people of this land, I alone will wear a cloak of moa feathers."

Toru nodded and water dripped from his grey hair. "The claws will hold much power. We will wear them over our hearts."

"No claws for me." Manunui thrust out his chest. "I will have a necklace of its teeth."

They laughed, for they knew there was no such thing as a moa's tooth.

Hunter turned away. He knew how quickly their laughter could turn to anger. He studied the shining stones of the beach, the black water flecked with rain. He could run. He could swim. But that was not enough. Other slaves had tried to run away, and the young men of the village had been sent out to search for them. Be it days or months, the chase went on until the runaway was found. That is how they were, these people. They never gave up, and when the slaves were brought back, a slow death awaited them. They were buried alive, or hung by the feet over a smoking fire as a warning to others. Hunter knew he would need to find a place of refuge from which he could never be taken.

Two summers past, something unexpected happened. Some *huhu* men came from another land. They settled beyond this valley, near the entrance of the next sound, where they killed and butchered seals. Hunter heard about them, men who had skin as white as the huhu grubs that burrowed in rotten logs, and who could kill at a distance, with thunder spears. They were wasteful, these huhu men, throwing away good seal meat and taking the skins to their homeland on their giant canoes hung with wind-catchers.

But it was said that in their camp they had many things of great wonder. Hunter saw the huhus for himself when they visited the village. They gave the people needles not of albatross bone, but of a rock Hunter had not seen before, as hard as flint and as bright as water. There were spearheads they called copper nails, hard, the colour of clay. Chief Te Hauwai was given a soft basket to wear upside down on his head to keep off rain and sun. The people had laughed with him. Who would want to be protected from the smiles and tears of Rangi, the sky father? And the head basket, turned upside down, was used to store bone for carving.

The huhu men left these things and more in exchange for *peruperu,* the purple potato, and mats made from flax and rushes.

Later, the warriors talked amongst themselves of sending a raiding party to the camp of the huhu men and taking all their things of great wonder. But talk had died from fear of the thunder spears, which could spit fire and make a hole as big as a fist in a man's chest.

Hunter had seen some good in the eyes of the huhu

man who had brought the copper nails. On the huhu's third visit to the village, Hunter had been lifting potatoes with his digging stick when the man approached him. This huhu had looked at Hunter eye to eye and touched his hand, palm to palm, bringing displeasure to Te Hauwai and wonder to Hunter's heart.

To the huhu, the no-name was not a slave but a man of equal status, and this caused a plan to grow in Hunter's mind. When the moment was as ready as a hatching egg, he could escape to the camp of the huhu men and they would take him with their sealskins back across the sea to their homeland.

Te Hauwai coughed and spat on the ground. "The old ones told stories of moa twice the height of a man."

Manunui nodded. "Strong, strong. One hit from the giant beak can put a hole through a hunter's skull." He rubbed his head as though feeling the pain.

Hunter listened, hearing weakness in their breathing. Running away now would be an easy thing. By the time these old men sent out a search party, he would be safe with the huhu, who would protect him with their thunder spears. It was a good plan. He could be out of their sight before they rose to their feet. Indeed, he could.

But the desire to run away did not travel from his head to his legs. Soon, but not yet, his heart said. At this moment the only readiness in him was for the giant bird that stalked the valley of his visions.

He closed his eyes to the rain and again felt the moa

moving inside him. The limitless darkness inside his eyelids showed him the moa's great eye very close, and he thought that the moa was probably like himself, the last of its kind. The red-rimmed eyes, golden with light, seemed to stare directly into his thoughts. He shook his head, blinked a couple of times. The bird's eye disappeared. The air shivered with rain, and there was a new vision in front of him.

Hanging thin as a veil of mist between the cloud and the mountain was a great white canoe that slid through the sky with wings outstretched like an albatross's. Perhaps it was a bird, for it was calling in a low voice that rattled like falling stones. Hunter had seen nothing like it before. Then, as quickly as it had come, the shape rippled, disappeared, and was replaced by yet another vision.

In the rain-streaked air, as pale as moonlight, there shimmered a young huhu woman with white hair and eyes as blue as sky. She wore a rainbow around her neck, an omen of good fortune, yet her eyes were wide with desperate fear. As Hunter watched, her terror spread to the rest of her face and then beyond, rippling the air until it washed, ice-cold, on his own skin. For an instant her fear was his, a frost around his heart, then she was gone and there was only the rain, like small stones bouncing on the black water, and the smell of wetness everywhere.

"Go!" commanded Te Hauwai, standing, leaning on his spear.

Hunter slowly rose, head bowed, and, turning his back to the sea, led the way into the valley of the moa.

2 0 0 5

Mum was right about Aunt Allie. She was all over the place like a grasshopper, making toast, painting her nails purple, watering potted plants, trying to phone her hairdresser, smudging her nails, jiving around, and singing love songs because she was going to see her American boyfriend.

Whatever mood Aunt Allie was in, she filled the entire house with it. Jordan and her brothers had learned on the first day of their holiday in Wellington that you stood back and left Aunt Allie to it. She organised everything and everyone, and most of the time that was pretty cool.

"You'll enjoy staying with Allie," Mum had told Jordan. "She's your age, a thirty-four-year-old teenager."

"Thanks heaps," Jordan had replied, but after a week with Aunt Allie, she knew exactly what Mum meant. There were times when Jordan felt ancient compared to Aunt Allie, and times when her mother's youngest sister seemed like Jordan's twin.

Robbie and Baxter adored Aunt Allie. Who else would take them to a restaurant and only look at the dessert menu? Jordan had felt a weight of responsibility as her brothers teetered between chocolate cheesecake and blackberry pie. She'd gotten as far as "I don't think Mum—" when Aunt Allie shot back, "Your mum isn't here, so she can mind her own beeswax. Relax, kiddo, pudding doesn't give you pimples."

"Into gear, haystack!" Aunt Allie ruffled Robbie's hair. "Bathroom, comb, toothbrush, look under your bed. If I find your pajamas, I'll give them to the Salvation Army. Want another doughnut, Baxter? Sure. Take your pick. Jordan, all the Christmas presents are in the blue bag. Swiss Army knife for your father, so it's got to be checked luggage. If you carry it on, they'll confiscate it. Sweetie, that pink top suits you. Your mother used to wear pink. Red was my—Hell's bells, excuse my French, look at the time! Baxie boy, eat it in the car. *We're not here.*"

It wasn't much of a day. Heavy cloud, cold wind. On the way to the airport, Jordan sat in the front seat, glancing at Aunt Allie, who sang and tapped her purple nails on the steering wheel. She was gorgeous, Jordan had to admit. She looked more Maori than their mother, with great skin and large, cheeky eyes that were a mixture of brown and grey. Her listening skills weren't up to much, but she really liked kids and she'd gone out of her way to give them a good time—movies, museum, boat ride, go-carts, zoo, a pony trek, heaps of junk food. Baxter and Robbie had been in heaven.

"This time tomorrow you'll be with John," Jordan said.

"Today," said Aunt Allie. "You forget the date line, honey. I arrive in Los Angeles before I leave Auckland. How's that for fast work?"

Jordan had forgotten the international date line, off the east coast of New Zealand. When you crossed that, you lost twenty-four hours. She took her new scarf out of her jacket pocket. "What's John like?"

Aunt Allie gave her a confidential girl-to-girl look. "Dishy! His mother's Italian. *Buon giorno! Amore! Hasta la vista,* baby!"

"Spanish," Jordan said. She'd bought the scarf with her own money. All her holiday savings on one thing. But no one in Invercargill would have a scarf like this. Her friends would drop dead backwards, screeching with envy.

"No," said Aunt Allie. "She comes from Naples. *Macaroni, fettucine,* real *Italiano.* Her sons have American names."

Jordan wound the fabric around her neck. It was fabulous, rainbow-dyed silk, dozens of shades running into each other. "*Hasta la vista* is Spanish," she said.

"Are we Italian?" Robbie was leaning forward from the backseat.

"No," said Jordan. "Do up your seat belt. Dad's part Ngati Porou—"

"You're Ngati Bittsa," said Aunt Allie. "Bittsa this, bittsa that."

Jordan began again. "We're Maori—Ngati Porou and Arawa as well as Swedish, English, Scottish, Irish, and German."

"Just like I said." Aunt Allie waved her hand. "Ngati Bittsa. Now, Ngati Urban, that's me. You"—she looked at

Jordan—"you're Maori on the inside, Swedish on the outside, dead spit of Great-gran Inger. They said her hair was so blond, no one noticed when it went white. Have you got those tickets?"

"Of course." Jordan looked at the grey sky and the ruffled water of Evan's Bay. The forecast wasn't good, but at least the wind wasn't as bad as it had been when they'd arrived. Their Boeing had jerked and flapped its wings like a frantic seagull until the last few seconds before it landed, and Robbie had been on the point of throwing up.

"The rest of you is Maori." Aunt Allie waggled purple-pointed fingers at Jordan. "You're like your mother. Can't keep your shoes on."

"What?" Jordan felt her face grow warm from anger and embarrassment. "What do you mean?"

"It's this Papatuanuku thing," said Aunt Allie. "Got to stay bonded with old Mother Earth. Your mum always said her feet starved in shoes."

Jordan nodded as her wave of anger receded. It was true enough. She and Mum suffered from hot, restless feet that were soothed by contact with the earth. Nothing was more delicious than standing in dew-soaked grass, or soft sand, or garden soil that came up damp between the toes. Wearing shoes was like wearing gloves. It put a barrier between you and the world.

"All that genealogy stuff leaves me cold," said Aunt Allie.

Jordan sat higher and crossed her legs. In the middle

of the year she had started a family genealogy project, trying to reclaim her Maori heritage. She still hadn't finished it. Her parents weren't much help. Although Mum wasn't as flippant as Aunt Allie, she didn't have time to get all tribal, she said, and besides, she'd forgotten most of the language. Dad reckoned that genealogy was important. "Good for you, girl. That'll keep you busy for the rest of your life." But he wasn't interested in his culture for himself. "I'm just a twenty-first-century Kiwi," he said, waving history away with a flick of his bony knuckles, and she had wanted to yell at him, Yes, but what do you feel inside?

She glimpsed the airport, the control tower, an orange windsock waving like the trunk of an angry elephant. She turned to Aunt Allie. "Everything we have comes from the past. Think about it. If we don't know our ancestors, how do we know who we are? We're like rootless trees!" Then she thought, Oh, stink, now she'll be mad at me and I'll get one of her famous lectures.

But her aunt could not be deflated. "I'm just saying it's not my thing," she replied. "Robbie, when we get to the parking lot, you and Baxter grab two trolleys for the luggage. You said you had the tickets? Brilliant. Remember, you change planes at Dunedin. Wellington to Dunedin and then Dunedin to Invercargill. Your father's meeting you. Don't get lost."

"I am fourteen," Jordan reminded her.

"No, you're not," said Baxter.

"Nearly fourteen," said Jordan. "I think I can get us off one plane and onto another. Don't worry, Aunt Allie. Dad will ring to let you know we've arrived." She looked sideways at her aunt. "You know what Dad says? He says genealogy is important."

Aunt Allie laughed as she swung the car into the parking lot. "Sweetie, stick your ancestors up your sweater, and tell your dad not to call me. By the time you get to Invercargill, I'll be on my way to Auckland, and in line for good old Californ-eye-ay. *La dolce vita*. Hasta la vista, baby!"

Jordan looked out the window at the airline departure terminal. The sky was a bowl of cloud soup and the New Zealand flag flapped and rattled against its pole. She sighed and looked back at Aunt Allie's smiling lipstick. Stink! she thought. How could a woman who owned a successful computer business be so insensitive? She took a deep breath. "My Maori studies teacher says our ancestors are the threads that make up the tapestry of our lives. I believe him. That's what I really believe."

The purple smile didn't flicker. "Yeah, yeah, kiddo. I believed everything, too, when I was your age."

The instant they stopped, the boys tumbled out of the car and ran to get trolleys. Robbie's hair was on end and his open jacket flew back off his shoulders. Baxter, six, but short for his age, tried to keep up on those silly thick-soled shoes Aunt Allie had bought him. Jordan didn't know what her parents would say about them. They were stilts, more like it. Baxter thought the extra height was cool. He leaned on the handle of the trolley as though he were a giant disguised as a dwarf, and when he saw them watching, he put out his tongue. Typical Baxter. Always playing for laughs.

Aunt Allie blew him a kiss. "Smart little brat."

There was no laughing when they discovered that their flight had been cancelled. They stood at the check-in counter, their bags heaped on the weighing platform, while Aunt Allie tapped her purple nails. "What do you mean, cancelled?"

"I'm sorry. Engineering requirements." The attendant, who was probably not much older than Jordan, looked at her computer. "They had some trouble with the plane and it's being serviced. I can put all three on the next available flight."

"When is that?" Aunt Allie asked.

"Tomorrow morning."

"Tomorrow morning!" The purple nails rattled like hailstones. "These kids have to be back in Invercargill today. Forget the available. Put them on the next flight!"

"I'm sorry." The girl shook her head as she stabbed at her computer. "It's nearly Christmas."

"I know it's nearly stuffing Christmas!" Aunt Allie swung on her black high heels. "But they've got booked return tickets. See? See this? They go back this morning, end of story!"

The girl looked as though she might cry. "I'm really very sorry. These things can't be avoided."

"They're kids!" Aunt Allie got loud. "If you want to bump someone off a flight, try the big people who can look after themselves."

"I—I can give you a voucher for the extra night's accommodation," the girl said.

"You're not listening to me! I said these children have to go home today! I'm flying to Auckland this afternoon. I'm leaving the country tonight. Who's going to baby-sit them? You?"

"Excuse me," said the girl, and she ran behind the counters into a doorway marked PRIVATE.

An older woman came out, square-shaped, grey hair, face set in a map of lines, firm but not unfriendly. Aunt Allie tried pleading with her. "It's not a matter of money. I'll pay. Put them in first class."

The woman looked at the computer. "Nope. Every seat on every flight to Dunedin is booked, and there are no extra flights today." She smoothed back her hair with both hands, then glanced up at Aunt Allie. "All I can suggest is a charter."

"Charter?"

"A private charter. There are small planes that do this sort of work. The cost varies. Would you like me to enquire for you?"

Aunt Allie was now leaning against the counter, her chin in her hand. She took a full breath that raised her shoulders, and then huffed it out in a loud sigh. "Okay," she said. "Okay, go ahead."

The clouds were heavy, sinking lower, and the wind breathed smells of sea in their faces. Jordan's silk scarf unwound, slithered from her neck, and might have been blown clear across the parking lot had not Baxter run after it in his ridiculous shoes. He waved it like a banner. "Where's my reward?"

"Give it to me!"

"I want a reward! It's worth it."

"Okay." Jordan grabbed him. "One big kiss!"

"Yuck!" Baxie squirmed in her grasp. "That's not a reward. That's punishment."

"You asked for it!"

"Leave him alone, Jordan!" Robbie came between them. "You know he hates that!"

Jordan shrugged. She knotted the silk around her neck and walked backwards against the wind, watching Aunt Allie, who trotted toward them with her thumb in the air. She was signalling she'd booked a small plane.

"Yay!" cried Baxter. "We're going!"

Robbie looked a question at Jordan.

Jordan swallowed. "Great. We'll be home before dark."

They wheeled their luggage to the car, reloaded, and followed a road at the back of the airport to some white-painted hangars and a creaking sign that said PEGASUS AVIATION. Aunt Allie told them to wait while she went into the office.

There was silence in the car, then Robbie said what they were all thinking. "I hope we're not going in one of those!"

The planes looked like toys. There were three parked in a line, all the same, small wings, a toy propeller, a door on each side, the name PEGASUS and a number painted in black near the tail.

"Cessnas," Baxter said.

Jordan wrapped her arms around herself, feeling sudden coldness. The eternal wind, the *hau* of her ancestors, was blowing right through her. They didn't have to go. Aunt Allie had heaps of friends. What about the nice people who worked in her office? Someone could give them beds for the night and put them on a big plane tomorrow.

"I'll be sick," Robbie warned.

"I've got an idea," Jordan told him. "We can stay—"

But at that moment, Aunt Allie came out of the Pegasus office, and it was obvious they had no choice. She walked with a tall orange-haired man in grey overalls, and the way she leaned against him, anyone would think he was a new boyfriend.

Baxter flattened his nose against the glass. "Is he the pilot?"

Jordan hugged her arms. Her teeth were chattering so hard, she couldn't answer. The wind was too cold for summer. It came from another season and it bore a strange smell, old and dark. She saw the man walking toward the car and she had a strong urge to lock all the doors.

It was Aunt Allie who pulled open Jordan's door. "Darlings, I want you to meet Harold. He's going to take you all the way to Invercargill."

The man had an orange mustache and eyebrows. He looked at Aunt Allie and winked. "Only if you come, too."

Baxter leaned forward, his face almost in Jordan's hair. "What about John Borno?"

Jordan turned and their noses met. "It's Buon Giorno!"

His smile was triumphant. Of course he knew that. She'd walked right into his trick.

She pushed him back on his seat and waved her fingertips at him. "Hasta la vista, baby brother."

CHAPTER THREE

1 8 0 5

As the hunting party moved inland, the low-bellied clouds glittered with ragged lines of fire that spread and sizzled over the valley. Lightning was the *moko* of Rangi, decided Hunter, the tattoo on the face of the sky god. Almost immediately, a boom of thunder shook his ears. He stopped and glanced at Manunui-a-te-maunga behind him. The man had turned to speak to his companions and Hunter could not hear their words for the rattle of rain. Aiiee! How that water fell! The tears of the sky father weeping for earth mother Papatuanuku rapidly grew into a great storm of grief. Falling water filled the air with grey lines so that the trees, the valley, and the mountains on either side were hidden.

Te Hauwai called to him. "We will make a camp for the night."

Hunter bowed his head in reply. Te Hauwai knew the cave, farther into the trees. He led the way, pausing so that Hunter could beat aside the scrub and nettles blocking the path. More lightning lit the sky with lines of fire. Hunter felt Manunui jump. The men were not cowards, but they believed in omens and this was not good, this sudden fierce storm as they entered the valley of the moa.

Hunter was not afraid of omens. He could read the ways of earth and sky. He knew their voices as his own. Fear surely belonged with that which was not understood. As he pulled back tree branches to let the men past, thunder roared over their heads, as though the sky were falling, and Te Hauwai sucked in his breath. "Aiee! It is a storm of storms!"

The cave was dry although water fell over the front of it to form a shallow stream amongst the moss and ferns. They bowed under the new waterfall, went inside, and shook themselves. The three warriors sat on the higher ground at the back of the cave while Hunter looked for fire sticks to prepare a fire. He knew that caves were often used for shelter by hunting parties. It was a way of being that whoever used a camp left fire sticks and some dry wood for the next hunting party.

Hunter found sticks and dried moss in a recess, but there was not much wood. With a flint, he notched one stick and cut a point in the other. Then he began the long task of fire-making, whirling the upright stick in his hands to create friction and heat. It was the task of a slave and he had done it many times. His hands worked by them-selves as he stared out through the lines of water at the bush outside. Ferns, weighed with water, bowed to the earth. Mosses hung like long wet hair.

Hunter's thoughts were not with the storm but with the girl he had seen in his daydream, his moe-mahi. With-out doubt she was a huhu, or a *pakeha,* as the tribe called them. Why had she come to him? Her hair and face were the palest he'd seen, the colour of moonlight. *Marama.* That is what he should call her. Moonlight girl. Why had she come to him, and what was the fear that had jumped across his vision to make bumps on his own skin? The *waka,* the white canoe bird that flew above the moun-tains—what was that?

The familiar smell of hot wood came from the fire sticks. His hands, too, were hot inside their hard skin from the ceaseless rubbing, whirling. He saw a small curl of smoke from the moss under the pointed stick.

At the back of the cave, the men talked through full

mouths. Safe from the storm, they were eating the potatoes and yams from their baskets. They would not throw any to the no-name, but Hunter did not care. There was much to eat beyond the cave. At the far end of the beach were *kuku,* little mussels soon uncovered by the tide, limpets, seaweed. Storm or no storm, he would gather a full store of seafood. The men would cook it, and when they had finished eating, he would have what was left.

The smoke increased under his breath and the point of the stick glowed red. He heaped more moss over the ember. Gently, steadily, he blew on it. The smoke became thicker and rose into his eyes, then a tongue of flame appeared. He sat back on his haunches and, with his flint, shaved some bark and wood off a dry branch. A few heartbeats later, a small, strong fire crackled at the mouth of the cave. He looked back at Te Hauwai, lowered his head, and stretched his hands to indicate that he was going out for firewood. In a good mood, Te Hauwai laughed and threw him a flax basket. "We will get the firewood. You bring back a moa to roast."

Hunter bowed and went out into the wet.

The lightning and thunder had moved toward the coast, but the tears of the sky father were still heavy. When he was young, Hunter often stood out in the rain to find comfort from Rangi's grief. Many times he had heard the story of sky father and earth mother, how they had been forced apart by their sons, and how sky father had wept on sky mother. So had he, the no-name, been snatched from his place of belonging. So had he cried in the night for something he no longer remembered. The tears of sky father Rangi had become his tears.

In the village of his captors, he answered to calls of "slave" and "no-name." He kept his head bowed and he slept in the dust with the dogs, but in his mind he stood as tall as an ancient *totara* tree. The slave child was now a man who had given himself the name Hunter, son of Tane, the god of the forest, who was born of Rangi, the sky father, and Papatuanuku, the earth mother. This was the ancestry he claimed for himself while bowing on the outside and standing tall on the inside. Hunter. No one would take his name from him, for he would never speak it, never allow another to use it.

The tide was still far out, which was good, for the beach was narrow, dropping away to a great depth a few paces from the low watermark where kelp lay in thick ribbons. With his flint he cut away soft new growth of kelp, thanking it for its goodness as he put it in the basket. He gave thanks for the little black mussels as he wrenched them from the rocks. One of the mussels he placed between his teeth, bit hard, and cracked for bait. Then he unwound the flax cord, both bird snare and fishing line, from the sealskin at his waist. Tied to one end of the line was a hook carved from the bone of a whale. He slid a narrow stone weight between the threads of the braided cord and wound the outer rim of mussel meat around the hook.

Ankle-deep in the kelp, he dropped the line into the dark, rain-spotted water until it rested on the steep bank amongst the seaweed. Almost at once, the cord jerked in his hand and he pulled up a wriggling cod. Carefully he took the hook from the fish's mouth and returned it to the sea. It was a way of being, that the first fish caught should always be given back to Tangaroa, god of the sea, and since the cod had swallowed his bait, Hunter needed to bite open another mussel.

The next cod came up jumping, splashing, as thick as his arm. He swung it onto the beach, thanked it, bit it on the head to kill it, and put it in the basket. Fishing in these waters was easy with many cod and *terakihi* close to the shore. Before the sky had finished groaning and weeping, the basket was full of food from the sea. Hunter wound the flax cord around his waist, then heaved the handles of the basket over his shoulder, feeling the weight of fish against his back. Two steps and he paused, sensing something more than fish, more than rain. The dark water and misted mountains rippled before his eyes so that light and shadow became mixed as in a dream. Through the ripples, at the other end of the small bay, he saw not the moa but the waka, that strange white canoe with featherless wings. This time it was on the beach. At first it appeared thin as mist. He could make out the rocks and trees behind it. Then the image grew stronger, a solid canoe, its prow in the bush, its stern in the sea. Sitting in the front was the huhu warrior who had paddled it to this bay.

Beside the huhu was the girl of moonlight.

As Hunter squinted to see more clearly, the waka began to slide backwards into the water. It did not float. For a little while it sat half in and half out of the tide, then slowly it slid under, releasing bubbles as it disappeared into the depths. The bubbles ceased, the ripples flattened. The vision changed shape and he was back on the stony, rain-washed beach with the flax kit, heavy with seafood, dripping against his back.

He marvelled at what he had just seen. Rangi, god of the heavens, had given his sky canoe to his son Tangaroa, god of the sea. But why? What was the meaning of this moe-mahi for Hunter? He stood still long after the vision had cleared, hoping that he would see the moon girl again, but she did not appear. Did she now live under the sea? Had she drowned?

CHAPTER FOUR

2 0 0 5

Jordan thought sky and earth could be reversed. They were the same concrete grey color. On this side of the runway, the parked planes bounced on their wheels, wingtips flexing in the breeze, like anxious birds.

Baxter was the only one who wanted to go on the Cessna. "I'm sitting in the front!" he cried as he reached high on his platform soles for the handle. "I'm telling the pilot what to do." The cockpit door swung open and he would have jumped into the seat next to the pilot's except that it had a clipboard and some papers on it. He waited, with one hand on the door, for Harold to come out of the Pegasus office. Robbie stood farther away with Jordan and the bags. Already he looked sick.

Jordan's smile twitched with effort. "He's filing the flight plan. That's what they have to do. He can't just fly anywhere he likes, because—" She stopped, but it was too late. Robbie's big eyes grew bigger as his thoughts finished the sentence.

"If he crashes, they have to know where to look," he said.

Jordan repeated what Aunt Allie had told them: "Small planes are safer than big jets." She tried to sound convincing, but words were weightless, and she wished that she'd grabbed Aunt Allie's cell phone to call Mum and Dad. She knew, absolutely knew, that their parents wouldn't want them flying the full length of the South Island on this silly little aircraft that looked like a toy, the kind of thing Robbie would assemble from a kit, with plastic and glue.

Aunt Allie said she would ring their parents just as soon as she'd finished at the hairdresser's. Jordan knew what the conversation would be like. Mum would be upset and would shout over the phone. Heaven help us! she would say. Alison, what next!

Harold the pilot lost his smile the minute Aunt Allie drove away, and Jordan soon realised that kids weren't on his list of favourite people. When he came striding out of the office, he took one look at Baxter holding the cockpit door open. "I thought I told you not to touch anything!"

Baxter went red. His mouth opened, but no sound came out.

"He didn't touch anything," said Jordan. "He just wants to know if he can sit in front."

Harold wrenched the door out of Baxter's grasp and slammed it. "If he didn't touch it, how come it opened? You wave a magic wand or something? All of you, get in the back. Round this side."

Jordan went first, holding on to Baxter, who was ready to cry. Harold opened his door and pushed the seat forward. Jordan climbed in, then Baxter and Robbie. Harold passed them the four bags to go in the luggage space behind their seats—three soft cargo bags and the blue canvas satchel with Aunt Allie's Christmas presents. Jordan thought that if the plane bounced up and down, there would be nothing to stop the luggage from coming out and landing on top of them, but she didn't complain. The pilot smelled of hot sweat, a strong, angry smell, and people could make mistakes when they were in that mood. He put his seat back, hopped in, and told them to fasten their harness.

"Harness?" Robbie looked at the cabin roof.

"Seat belts!" snapped Harold. "Put your arms through the loops and fasten them across your chest. It's not all that difficult."

"Oh." Robbie put his arms through the straps. Already, he had a paper sick bag in his right hand. "Sorry. Thank you."

Jordan gave him a small, patient smile. Poor old Robbie. He was always so polite, but sometimes it wasn't necessary. Dad talked like that, a born peacekeeper who apologised when someone bumped into him. Jordan and Baxie took after Mum's side of the family, although none of them was quite as pushy as Aunt Allie.

Harold reached out to click some switches. "There are magazines in the seat pockets. Put them back when you've finished. It's three hours to Christchurch. We'll refuel, then head on down to Invercargill. Weather's okay. There's a front coming in tonight, no worries, we'll be well ahead of that. Get you to Invercargill about four." He turned to look at Jordan. "Is your aunt married?"

"No," said Jordan. "But she's got a boyfriend."

"Serious or not serious?"

"Serious. That's why she's going to America."

Harold's face went from shadow to sunlight. "So he lives over there and she lives over here? Okay, okay!" He started the engine and the plane shook all over like a wet dog. "She's a cool chick, your aunt!" he bellowed over the noise.

Jordan looked out the side window as the plane rolled down the tarmac. The main runways on her left were occupied with big Boeings flying to every part of the country. Stink! This is a big mistake. They could have taken another route on one of the big planes. There had to be flights with spare seats. It was typical of Aunt Allie to grab the first suggestion offered. She didn't consult them, didn't even phone Mum and Dad. It was all hasta la vista, baby!

Robbie was looking at Jordan and saying something she couldn't hear over the engine. She leaned across Baxter to get her ear close to Robbie's mouth.

"It's going to be all right," Robbie said.

She realised that she'd been scowling. She smiled. "Of course it'll be okay," she shouted back.

They took off to the south, the plane rising unsteadily over the runway and then the sea. Jordan looked down at the ruffled water, grey as steel, the far hills with houses stuck like postage stamps in an album, the wispy grey cloud between them and the sun. Slowly the knots in her stomach relaxed and her breathing became even. The takeoff had been wobbly, but now that they were flying high and level over Cook Strait, the plane was as steady as a car on a highway. Even Robbie sat up straight, face against the window, hand relaxed on the sick bag.

"I can't see!" cried Baxter, wriggling his dissatisfaction at being in the middle.

Jordan groped in the seat pocket for something to stop

his fussing. Baxie never sat still for long. There were a couple of aviation magazines in the pocket. They would suit him fine. Jordan put them on his lap. "You can have the window seat after Christchurch."

As they flew over the South Island coast, she allowed herself the small thought that this flight could become enjoyable. Her fear dissolved in the beauty of the morning, with the passing of steep cliffs, lines of dark trees, houses, green vineyards, sheep scattered like grains of rice on rounded hills, roads that wound through it all, stitching the land with single strands of grey thread.

The plane was the size of a very small car, yet the word *waka* kept coming into her head. Why *waka*? Maybe the plane was more like a canoe. Yeah, right. The air flowed like water, and the land beneath them was like the bottom of the sea. She remembered the chant she'd learned at school in Maori studies. *Toia mai, he waka!* Haul up your canoe! It could mean many things, but mostly it was a chant for coming home. She looked through the front windshield. The Cessna's paddle was a whirring circle of propeller in this bright sea of air. *Toia mai, he waka.* Yes, it was a canoe, taking her to the land where her heart had its nest. The feeling of homecoming grew strong in her. She leaned back against the seat and smiled at the fear that had made her shiver with cold. One week to Christmas. Tomorrow, they'd probably go out to Pearson's farm for the Christmas tree, and Jordan would jam a chair against her bedroom door while she wrapped her presents for her family. She'd bought the presents way back in September and hidden them on top of the wardrobe. For her best friend, Cathie, there was an imitation diamond nose stud that would surely draw a comment from Mum. Jordan couldn't wait for that to happen. Mum was always going on about Cathie getting her nose pierced. Self-mutilation, she called it. Well, I've got news for you, Mum, Jordan would say. Your sister Allie's got a bar through her belly button.

For Baxie, she had a book of knock-knock jokes, and for Robbie, a book about space flight. Maybe she should swap them. Robbie suffered from a serious lack of humour, and a book on outer space might help Baxie realise he wasn't the centre of the universe. Nah, she told herself. Button up the mean streak, Jordan. They're your brothers, and they're better than most. *Toia mai. He waka.* Happy Christmas. We're going home.

CHAPTER FIVE

1 8 0 5

Hunter stirred with the harsh call of the moa in his ears. He opened his eyes and the call faded. By the time he was fully awake, there was no sound other than deep snores from the three old warriors and the drip of water at the front of the cave. He knew that the moa's call had been both inside and outside his head. The shrill cry had echoed along the valley as though the earth mother herself was wailing, and then came booming notes that Hunter recognised as a mating call. In his waking silence he searched for the meaning of this new discovery, and it came to him with clear truth. The moa knew its time was near. It had come to the valley in a search for a mate who would nest and lay eggs full of new life. What Hunter had heard in his sleep was a desperate cry for the survival of a species.

He rolled over and saw, in the glow of the dying fire, water falling over the entrance, each drop lit like a speck of blood. Beyond was a blackness that whispered with a thousand wet voices, even though the rain itself had stopped. He let his ears search the darkness beyond water sounds and the grunting breath of the men. He sat up and rested his arms on his knees.

The three warriors slept well, so sure of his obedience that they did not keep guard or tie his ankles as they had when he was younger. They ruled through fear and had grown confident in his submissiveness, seeing him as one of their tools—like an eel trap or an adze. It would be easy to leave them right now. He could walk away and they would not stir. By dawn he would be at the other end of the valley. Another day and he would reach the huhu men and find protection. The bird also would be safe. What was still stopping him?

The answer was lack of readiness. The plans in his

head leaned forward into the darkness, but his heart was held as though in a net of vines, and he had to wait until the moment of inner freedom when his heart said, *Now!* Besides, he knew that his escape would not guarantee the safety of the great bird. These old men would not find the moa on their own, but they would return with a crowd of young warriors who would not rest until they had encircled the great bird with traps. The destiny of the moa was carved into the land. It was his own future that had been made uncertain. The new visions of the sky waka had somehow made a prisoner of his heart.

"Marama," he whispered as he lay down again, his back to the fire. "Marama, girl of the moon."

The morning was hung with clouds but there was no rain. The land ran with water as though it had just risen from a lake, and the sound of fast-flowing streams hid the songs of birds. Hunter ate what the men had left from their meal, and laid bones and empty mussel shells in a hollow under a tree. He cleared the fire, put some moss and brushwood with the fire sticks in the cave recess, and then sat on his haunches outside to wait for the three old warriors.

The mana of each man was significant: Te Hauwai was the chief, the father of the village; Manunui-a-te-maunga was directly linked to the ancient moa hunters of the tribe; and Toru had a skill with weapons, especially the axe, that was known across the land.

Hunter heard their voices now. They had wandered away from the cave and were squatting in the bushes for their morning requirements, grumbling at the sand flies that came in clouds to attack their tender parts.

Sand flies did not bother people of brown skin too much, except for the babies, but the huhu men, the pakeha at the seal camp, were a feast for every biting fly in these lands. The huhu who had come to the village and taken Hunter's hand, did so in gratitude. On his second visit, the man's pale flesh had been covered in red lumps. Hunter showed him how to cut a flax stalk, extract the jelly from the base, and rub it over his arms and face. He did so, and was pleased, this huhu man who wore strange garments, dirty and smelling bad. But his face was good, as were the sea-colour eyes that had looked at the slave. Hunter was sure he could trust him.

The sun pushed long fingers through the cloud, its touch warming the wet earth and drawing birdsong from the trees. The men came out of the bush, retying their seal-skins and talking amongst themselves. Toru pushed the handle of his famous greenstone adze through the cord at his waist and looked at Hunter, who quickly lowered his eyes.

"Go!" commanded Toru.

Hunter turned and led them along the bank of the flooded stream that ran through the valley. Because the way was strewn with boulders and fallen trees, he went slowly, aware that it was Toru, the warrior of the quick temper and the quick throwing arm, who was behind him. It was said that Toru never missed with that axe. Everyone knew what had happened to the man who had laughed at Toru and called him names. The man's laughter died with him and he had fallen with the axe handle sticking out of his head.

This morning, the warriors seemed to be in good spirits. The rain had cleared and Hunter had told them that the moa was near. They told each other stories of other hunts and of the deeds of their ancestors. Hunter listened to their laughter as he cleared the path for them, pushing aside dead branches and thorny scrub. Te Hauwai talked of his uncles but not of his father, Tirimai, who had been a great warrior. Hunter knew that Te Hauwai would never speak of Tirimai in his presence.

The story had come from others in the village, and over the years, Hunter had learned that the loss of his family, his slavery, were part of the payment for Tirimai's death.

Long ago, Hunter's people came from the northern land, Te-Ika-a-Maui, to seek *pounamu*, the greenstone that made fine clubs and adze heads. The pounamu seekers moved into the territory of Tirimai's people and Tirimai, with another man, challenged them. Hunter's father threw the spear that killed Tirimai. The other warrior escaped. He returned to the tribe and at once a war party had gone out to settle the debt. Only the child, the little no-name, survived.

He had grown up full of unspoken questions about his family. There were other slaves in the village who came from different tribes and who, like him, had no history, no status, no place of belonging. They could not help him.

As a young child, Hunter accepted being a no-name, but as his visions increased, he realised that he had a gift no one else shared. Who needed a moko, a tattoo, on his face when he bore Tane's own eyes within him? No one! He grew strong in this knowledge of himself, and while he was still a child, his crying at night ceased.

Another seeing came on him before the sun had risen from the cloud. It was neither the moa nor the huhu girl. This time, in front of his eyes, a duck sat in the middle of a clump of flax bushes, nine eggs beneath her feathers. He stopped, looked left and right. Yes, there was the flax, wet green spears at the edge of the stream. He squatted and pointed with his arm, and the men behind him were still. He signed with his hand and showed fingers for the nine eggs, expecting that they would tell him to reach into the clump. But it was Te Hauwai who advanced. He was quick, but not quick enough to catch the duck. She flew away clamouring, leaving a clutch of eggs.

Although they had eaten that morning, the men fell on the eggs, shook them against their ears to determine their freshness, and then cracked them into their mouths, three each. They laughed their pleasure.

"I expected an egg this big," said Toru, making a moa egg shape with his hands.

"Tonight you will have the whole bird," replied Manunui-a-te-maunga.

"Not the skin and feathers," added Te Hauwai, wiping his mouth with the back of his hand.

No one laughed at this, for they knew that a cloak made from the giant bird would make Te Hauwai greater than anyone in the land.

They pushed on, deep into the valley under a sky that threatened rain but did not deliver it. By midafternoon the trees had given way to low scrub, and mats of brown tussock grass were spread on stony ground. Here and there, they walked around a large lichen-covered boulder that had been left by an ancient glacier, but there were no signs of the moa. Hunter felt it, though. The hot smell was strong within him. He knew it was waiting.

"How much farther?" grumbled Manunui. The three warriors, already weary, had lost their good humour and their complaints rumbled like distant thunder.

The valley had narrowed and the mountains on either side were clear of mist so that the snow-spattered peaks were clearly visible. It was over one of these mountains that the white waka appeared to Hunter in a trembling of air. There was no warning. The sky shook as the canoe with wings came over the peak, down, down, over Hunter's head, and then, with a quick turn, it glided toward the sea.

The air grew thicker, filling his vision with movement. He shut his eyes for a moment and the face of the girl Marama was in front of him, long white hair, eyes and mouth open with fear. There were two children with her, smaller huhus with darker hair, and they, too, were caught in the same terror that washed over Hunter in a flood, filling his heart and making his skin as cold as snow. He blinked and shook his head. They disappeared.

"What is it?" demanded Toru. "What are you seeing?"

Hunter drew a deep breath and lowered his head. "The moa," he lied. "It is near."

"Where?" said Te Hauwai, changing his spear to his throwing hand.

"Very close," he said.

It was, after all, true, for a few steps later he noticed the broken branches of a bush and, beyond, a man-sized hole that had been scratched in the mud and stones. In spite of yesterday's rain, claw marks were still visible.

"Aiee!" breathed Manunui. He squatted by the hole and touched the gouged earth. "This was the work of no little chicken. It was made by a moa or a monster, a *taniwha*. One or the other is waiting for us."

The others knelt on the ground, examining the crater

as though it was sacred. Fingers with broken nails touched the grooves in the dirt, and Te Hauwai thanked his ancestors for bringing him to this honour.

"It is true," said Toru's voice, soft with wonder. "The moa still lives in this land."

Hunter's thoughts were not with the moa. His heart thumped like a crowd of running feet. Who were the girl of moonlight and the children with her, and what was their fear? Were they fairy people? Spirits sent by his dead ancestors? His head was full of wonderings, for there was no understanding at all in these new visions.

His skin was still cold with their terror. Although they appeared to him as huhus, no strangers could make such a demand on his heart. What he felt was deep in his blood. It was as though these huhus belonged to him.

CHAPTER SIX

2 0 0 5

Jordan woke as wheels bounced on the Christchurch runway. She hadn't intended to sleep. It just happened, and only for a few moments. She'd been staring at the flat farms of the Canterbury plains, her nose pressed against the window to avoid the pilot's cigarette smoke. Next thing, they'd landed. She looked at the boys, who grinned at her, pleased with the shift in seniority. Baxter shouted, "Have a nice nap?" and Robbie, not the least bit sick, blew some bubble gum at her.

Marama, thought Jordan. There had been a dream. She couldn't remember it, but a man had called her Marama and the weird thing was, somehow she knew his voice.

The plane stopped behind the main airport building and they sat while Harold ran down the engine. The whirring circle of the propeller slowed until it was a solid blade, the last switches were turned off, and Harold got out. He pulled his seat forward and told them to go into the office. "Toilets in there. Café with sandwiches, pies, drinks. You got money, I suppose."

Aunt Allie had given them ten dollars each, which they had planned to spend on something more interesting than food, but that had been after breakfast. Stomachs had short memories, Jordan decided, choosing two chicken sandwiches, an apple, and a bottle of water. Robbie bought a meat pie and a packet of potato chips, while Baxie insisted on having chocolate chip cookies and carrot cake. "Carrots are healthy," he told Jordan. "They've got vitamin C and stuff."

Jordan shook her head. "It's the sugar, Baxie. It's going to kill you stone dead."

"Yeah?" His teeth chomped the cake. "How can I be killed and not be stone dead?"

She brushed her jacket. "Stop spitting crumbs."

"Get moving!" Harold yelled at them from the doorway. He had refuelled the plane and was anxious to take off.

"We can eat on the plane," said Robbie, trying to be helpful.

"No way!" said Harold. "I'm not having it stinking of meat pies."

Why not? Jordan wanted to ask. It already stinks of cigarette smoke. But she said nothing because her mouth was full of sandwich and besides, making a pilot angry was definitely a risky business. She jammed the top back on the water bottle, put the apple in her jacket pocket, and told the boys to hurry up.

Outside, she zipped her jacket and turned the collar up to her ears. The cloud was low, spotting rain on the tarmac.

"Do you know how to spell the word *move*?" Harold stood by the plane, holding the door.

"Sorry," mumbled Robbie.

"We went as fast as we could." Jordan's voice was strong.

Harold dropped his cigarette and trod on it. "Fast isn't fast enough," he said. "There's bad weather coming from the southeast. I have to drop you in Invercargill and then get back ahead of it. Come on, come on!"

Robbie climbed across to the other side and Jordan sat in the middle, leaving the window seat behind the pilot for Baxter. Harold got in and pulled the door shut. "Harness!" he said. "How many times do I have to tell you?" He shook his head and Jordan noticed that the light shone pink through his ears. "So help me, I just love baby-sitting!"

Jordan pulled the straps over her shoulders. "You should have brought our aunt instead."

That made him smile. "Now you're talking," he said, flicking his ginger eyebrows. As he switched on the engine, he made another comment about Aunt Allie, but they couldn't hear it for the noise. Jordan was tall enough to see the instrument panel and the front passenger seat, which had on it a clipboard of papers, a book of maps— why did he need those?—a cigarette lighter, and a new pack of cigarettes. More horrible smoke, she thought. She'd just have to hold her scarf over her nose. What a pain! Her new scarf would stink of smoke, first wearing.

An hour out of Christchurch, the cloud grew thick around them and they lost sight of the ground. Squalls of rain exploded against the front glass and streaked across the side windows. The plane bumped as though the clouds were made of concrete. Jordan saw the green look around Robbie's mouth as she handed him a sick bag. He got it open just in time. Whether Harold liked it or not, the cabin filled with the warm smell of half-digested steak pie.

Harold didn't like it. He yelled something she couldn't hear above the roar of the engine, and waved his hand. Jordan thought he was telling them to throw the sick bag out of the window. They couldn't. The windows didn't open. She realised then that the pilot was pointing to the seat pocket. There was another bag there, plastic with a tie top. Harold wanted Robbie to put the paper sick bag in it so that the mess didn't spill over his plane. Robbie was too ill to do anything. Jordan took the steak pie bag from his stiff fingers, folded the top shut, and dropped it in the plastic rubbish container. She fastened the plastic bag and laid it on the floor between her feet. All this took time, for the plane bounced as though it were on a trampoline and sometimes her arms and hands seemed to float in the air without gravity. She hoped that the bag wouldn't get under their feet.

Robbie had grabbed a new sick bag and had it open, ready for the next installment. Jordan saw the fear in their eyes, which had become fixed and staring. She tried to appear calm, but her stomach had scrunched up tight, squeezing the chicken sandwiches. I won't be sick, she told herself, won't, won't, won't. She closed her eyes. *Waka*, she thought. *Marama*. Those words again, coming out of nowhere. She ignored them and prayed, Make this storm stop. Please, God, make it calm, make it clear.

The plane lurched and rattled. Something fell on her feet. It wasn't the plastic bag. It was the pilot's clipboard. Harold had his hand on the seat to steady the other things. In front of him, the radio receiver was swinging on its cord, part of its plastic covering broken. Harold grabbed the receiver, held it, shook it, and dropped it again. He turned his head and yelled something.

"What?" Jordan yelled back as she handed him the clipboard.

He repeated it, but she still couldn't hear. The grey cloud was streaking past them and the plane shuddered like a person with a fever.

Harold pulled the wheel back and they began to climb. The cloud became paler, thinner. Small rainbows appeared in the whir of the propellers.

Robbie was heaving into the second sick bag.

Sunlight came upon them so suddenly that it was like emerging from a hole in the ground. One second they were in cloud, the next, there was a brilliant blue sky above them and a sun that flared and dazzled with diamond light. The shuddering stopped. The plane flew steadily over a grey floor of cloud that looked as solid as ice.

Harold tried the radio handpiece several times before putting it back in its holder. He took off his headphones and his ears sprang out, freckled and red-rimmed. He lit a cigarette. A puff of smoke hit Jordan's face as he turned, his lips moving.

She leaned forward. "I can't hear!"

He yelled, "I said this front's come in early. Southeast! We're going over the mountains—west to get out of it. I'll get you as far as Te Anau."

She wasn't sure what he meant. "Aren't you flying us to Invercargill?"

He shook his head, the cigarette in the corner of his mouth. "Can't. Radio's gone. You'll have to get a bus."

A bus? Her mouth opened and she gasped. She leaned farther forward. "We don't have any money."

"You can phone your dad," he yelled. "I didn't order the weather, girlie. Look at that!" He pointed to the radio handpiece. "This is going to cost me more than it's costing you. Just be glad I'm not charging extra."

She sat back, wriggling to fit the space between her brothers. A phone call home. That was the answer. Te Anau was a long way from Invercargill, but, stink, after the rough stuff they'd just been through, travelling by road looked like a good option. It didn't matter how long they'd need to wait at the airport. She imagined Mum hugging and crying and saying, Oh, that Alison, and Dad worrying they might be cold, wet, hungry, sick. He was a real old fusser, Dad was. They both were.

These thoughts filled Jordan with comfort. She took the second sick bag from Robbie, reached down, and found the plastic rubbish container. Then she took a tissue out of her pocket and wiped the string of dribble that hung from the corner of his mouth. He gave her a weak smile.

Jordan remembered Robbie being born. Well, not being born exactly, because she'd started school about then, but she remembered seeing this cute little kid lying in Mum's arm with puke on his face. That was Robbie. Ultrasensitive stomach, just like the rest of him. Not Baxter, though. Baxie was as strong as a horse and could eat anything, especially sweet stuff.

Robbie leaned as far as his harness would allow. "I'm glad we're landing at Te Anau," he said.

The flight now was calm, a blue sky above with just a few wispy white clouds and a solid layer of grey cloud beneath. The droning of the engines made their eyelids heavy and they dozed, heads resting on each other. A beeping sound woke them. Jordan blinked. They were still flying in calm sunlight, but the alarm noise filled the cockpit, and on the instrument panel there was a red flashing light. The pilot was tapping it hard with the knuckles of his left hand.

"What's that?" she shouted at him.

His lips were moving, mostly around swear words.

Jordan reached across to touch his shoulder. "What's that light?"

"Fuel warning," he said.

CHAPTER SEVEN

1 8 0 5

They crossed the valley of scrub and tussock and were now in the forest that led to the next sound and the camp of the seal skinners. In this forest it was easy to track the moa. Hunter saw signs everywhere, broken twigs where leaves had been torn off, scratched earth, stones and dead wood turned over for bugs, rotten logs torn to bits.

Hunter stopped at a scratch hole so fresh that claw marks were still visible. In the hole lay a feather longer than his hand, dark brown and narrow. He crouched and pointed to it. Toru took it and passed it to Te Hauwai, who held it in two hands, a *taonga*, a precious thing to be admired in silence. Te Hauwai had two *huia* feathers on a cord through his ear. He inserted the moa feather into the cord between them and then stroked it from his ear to his shoulder. All of this Hunter saw from the edge of his eye, as he saw the smiles of the other two men. The warriors desired power and they would not be disappointed.

The floor of the forest was covered with mosses, ferns, small plants with starlike flowers, fungi, and dead branches scaled with lichen. Where the undergrowth had been scratched away, they saw claw marks and occasionally an entire footprint stamped in the mud. One time, Te

Hauwai stooped and, laying down his spear, spread his hand across a moa print. He could not cover it. He put his other hand alongside, but still the bird's foot was bigger. He became excited then. He stood up laughing and slapping his thighs. Turning to the others and then to the no-name, he did a surprising thing. He touched the slave. He jabbed his finger on the slave's shoulder. "The moa of your dreams is small. *Iti, iti!* See there?" he pointed to the ground. "This is my moa and it is big! *Nui, nui!*"

The others laughed, and Hunter kept still, his head down.

"The no-name has done well," chuckled Manunui-a-te-maunga.

Toru did not speak. With narrowed eyes he watched the slave, his hand resting easily on the handle of his axe. Hunter felt his spine tingle with threat, and his breath caught as though the air he inhaled had rough edges. He was glad when Te Hauwai gave the order to continue.

A few steps farther and they found another sign, the freshest yet. It was a heap of dark green excrement untouched by rain, so newly formed that a rank smell rose from it. Te Hauwai told the no-name to break it with a stick, and when he did so, they saw bones amongst the green digested fibre. This moa ate more than leaves and insects. The partial skeleton belonged to a bird. From the remains it appeared to have been a wood hen.

"*Weka,*" Te Hauwai said.

Manunui nodded. "Weka," he agreed, and there followed a silence. A weka was not a small hen. Clever and fast, it could easily outrun a man. The creature that had eaten it whole would surely be dangerous.

It was not for the slave to tell them that the moa had probably taken a wood hen that was injured or asleep. This great bird was old and was already seeing its own death as a certainty. The creatures of Tane knew the mysteries of life that were hidden from people, and they especially understood endings. It was the same with fish. Sometimes Hunter could put his hand in a stream and an eel would swim into it. Whales would hear the call of an ending and throw themselves onto a beach. Creatures understood that endings were also beginnings.

Above the smell of the manure, Hunter inhaled the dusty hot scent of the moa's feathers. He felt the beating of its heart alongside his.

Te Hauwai turned to him. "Is it close?"

He lowered his head. "It is but a breath away."

Te Hauwai said to the others, "We need to prepare ourselves."

They walked a little way to a fallen tree and sat in a row, silent, as was the way of being. Te Hauwai stood first, raised his arms, and spoke, gathering physical and spiritual strength from his ancestors. Then he asked the earth and the forest to help them. It was a long prayer. Manunui was next, followed by Toru. The moods of the journey, from complaints to laughter, had left them, and they were caught up in the sacred moment of the task to come.

Hunter, still squatting by the bird manure, felt their power. They were old warriors and their stomachs rested on their thin thighs, but their mana was that of mountains. From the edge of his sight, Hunter saw the three tattooed faces in a row, Manunui's lips folded over his gums, Toru with grey hair in his topknot, Te Hauwai's chest puckered with a long battle scar. The slave knew that all the experience these men had gathered had brought them to this moment. Killing the moa would be the most important thing in their lives.

The hot bird smell that washed over Hunter was so overpowering that his hands trembled. He stood up, left the men, and walked a little way into the bush. He paused, his hand on a low branch, and listened. There was nothing for his outer ear, but the ear inside him heard the heartbeat louder than his own. Soundlessly, he walked on, the green hair of lichen brushing his face as he passed under the branches of beech trees. The land sloped, rising toward the mountains, and a little farther on he would come to another clearing of tussock and small bushes. That's where it would be. When he closed his eyes, he could see it in his moe-mahi, walking slowly, head jerking on the long neck, old eyes alert. The bird's heartbeat was strong in his blood, its smell warm in his nose. Another few steps and he was at the edge of the clearing, under a young rimu tree.

He saw it.

The moa was no longer behind his eyes but in front of him, its brown-red feathers bright against the dark blue of the mountains, its neck curled like the new frond of a giant tree fern. It sensed him close and it stood absolutely still. Yet it was full of life, this great flightless bird, its head as high as a house post, small and smooth, with short feathers that grew longer down its neck. Its body was as round as a large rock, its scaly legs as thick as small trees. But the true strength of the moa lay in its powerful golden eyes. The red folds of skin around its eyes indicated a long life. How old, and where had it hatched? Not in this valley, or it would have been seen before this. Had it come over a vast landscape of mountains to die here, to answer a call like the whales on the beach? But it was still strong. Hunter's heart moved with strong feeling. Why should it be killed for the vanity of an old man?

He stepped into the clearing and strode toward it, sending his thoughts across the clear air between them. *Run! Run! You do not have to die this way. Go back into the mountains and be the master of your own ending.*

The bird stayed still, watching.

He waved his arms at it. *Go! Die with dignity. Let your spirit flow out in its own time, not through the bleeding holes of wounds.*

The moa did not move.

He wanted to shout the words in the voice of an avalanche, but could not without alerting the warriors. He went closer until his eyes were level with the bird's back, then he picked up a handful of small stones and threw them. Some bounced off the brown feathers. He saw the rapid closing of the eye membranes as the moa blinked, but that was all.

Hunter knew the bird understood him and he didn't know why it was not responding. *Go, go, go, go!* Eventually, he spread his arms wide and ran fast toward it.

The great bird moved. Its head swayed, it picked up its feet and broke into a lumbering run—but not toward the mountains. It cut a wide curve around Hunter, its claws raking the grasses, and headed into the forest, directly toward the warriors.

Hunter heard the breaking of twigs and then the shouting. He felt sick with frustration. His thoughts chased after the bird, crying, *You are not a slave! Your debt is not to men, but to freedom!*

He had changed nothing. Cries filtered through the forest, loud with triumph, and in his head he saw the moa bleeding into the earth, an axe in its side, a spear quivering in its breast. He felt helpless.

He put his hands to his head. Why had he not been able to save this creature? He closed his eyes, expecting to see a great beak flutter open in its last breath, a light go out in a golden eye. But it was not the moa he saw. In the endless sky behind his eyelids, a white waka fell and fell and fell. He punched his head to rid himself of the vision. Still the waka tumbled from a sky that shook with the screaming of children. Down they came, turning his bones to ice. He groaned and opened his eyes.

Who had said that the gift of seeing was a precious taonga, a treasure from Tane? It was not good. It was *makutu*, a curse that filled him with the troubles of others, as if he did not have hardship enough of his own. Seeing food was one thing, but often the visions went further than that. Who could understand the great weight of seeing death in the eyes of a child two days before a drowning? How could he say to a fellow slave, Tonight you will try to run away, but they will find you and cut you to pieces? As with the moa, he had tried many times to change what he had seen, and he had failed.

He glanced back toward the trees whose leaves stirred with death and the whooping cries of the warriors. Three old men and one old moa. Some epic battle! Te Hauwai would get his cloak and increase his mana, but the flesh would be too tough for eating. As for the seeing of the girl and the white waka, Hunter would not allow it to claim him. The vision was too big, and in his heart he knew it held the seeds of his own death. He would escape and make a new life for himself. *He was ready.*

He turned toward the head of the valley and ran with long easy strides, feeling the heat of freedom in him. The warriors would not catch him. He would work for the huhu seal skinners, and if the huhus beat him, it would be no worse than at the village. He'd bring the huhus fat shorebirds and eels, show them all the foods of forest and sea. In return, they would protect him with their thunder spears until their great waka came to take him away.

Halfway across the clearing, one of the sealskin wraps on Hunter's feet came loose and tripped him. He lurched forward and landed heavily, his breath knocked out of him, his knees and hands losing skin on the sharp stones. For a while he lay gasping, then, as he lifted himself to a kneeling position, he saw a shadow fall across the tussock to his left.

Slowly, Hunter turned his head.

Toru stood behind him, smiling, his bloodied axe in his hand.

CHAPTER EIGHT

2 0 0 5

The beeping noise stopped with the flick of a switch, but the red light on the instrument panel went on flashing.

Harold's head turned. "There's something wrong with the fuel gauge. We should still have half a tank. Don't worry. We'll make it to Te Anau."

Jordan reached out to Robbie and Baxter and at once they grabbed her hands. She could feel the heat of their palms against hers, and it was this, rather than the pilot's words, that consoled her. Mum once said that a family holding hands could beat an invasion by Mars. It was the afternoon they were walking home from the *Red Planet* movie, five of them hand in hand across the full width of a country road. Mr. Kroworz, the poultry farmer, coming toward them, had called out, "Do I have to jump this fence? Or is there a gate?" That's when Mum had laughed and said that thing about a family holding hands. It sounded silly then, but it felt true. It felt true now.

Their pilot put on his headphones. Jordan didn't know what he was listening to, but it meant she couldn't ask him questions. One thing, though, he had been right about the weather on the west coast of the South Island. They were still flying in sunshine and the solid mat of cloud beneath had thinned so that they could see ink-dark mountains and fingers of sea the colour of lead. There was no flat land, no airport or houses. Jordan took a deep breath. He knows what he's doing, she told herself. He's flown this plane hundreds of times. But the red light flashed brighter than the sunlight that splintered against the windows, and moisture squeaked on the palms of her hands.

Harold picked up the radio handpiece, tried it again, threw it down. He took off his headphones and yelled something at Jordan.

She leaned forward.

"You got a cell phone?" he wanted to know.

She shook her head.

He swore, then shouted at them, "If we don't get to Te Anau, it'll have to be Manapouri. No worries. We'll just drop a bit, have a look-see." He put the nose of the plane down, and the mountains below tilted toward them.

Jordan could see on the nearest peak a cap of hard snow that ran down, dirty grey, in the cracks. Below the stretch of bare rocks were some small bushes, and in the distance, larger trees to the water's edge. There wasn't even a boat on the sea. Where was Manapouri?

She felt Baxter's fingers tighten around hers with the same question. She looked at his face, pale under the freckles. He was crying. She put on a smile, but it was one of those smiles people made for cameras and it set as hard as cement. Robbie's hand had gone limp. He was staring at the flashing light, as though hypnotised. She squeezed his fingers, too, but he didn't respond.

"Fiordland," she said in his ear. "Isn't it beautiful?"

He didn't reply, and she didn't know why she'd said something so stupid. The scenery wasn't beautiful. Mountains like teeth. No flat land. It was terrifying.

The engine noise changed. The plane gave a huge cough, as though it were clearing its throat, roared, then coughed again. Harold snatched up the useless radio handpiece. Cough, cough. They felt the vibration in the floor, the walls, their seats. Baxter gave a sharp cry. They were still going down, level now with wisps of cloud.

Harold turned and yelled, "Check your harness! There's a nice little beach. Little Moon Bay."

Bay? What bay? Jordan rose in her seat to see through the front windows. There was no beach, just mountains and water. Steep mountains. Deep water. Now she knew it. They were going to crash. She looked at her brothers in their shoulder straps, saw their buckles fastened, saw her own. Baxie was screaming. Robbie's mouth and eyes were slack. She held on to their hands, thinking, waka, waka, waka, and then flat land came up under the nose of the aircraft, a sliver of light brown, curved like a fingernail between mountains and sea.

Harold was right. There was a beach.

The engine stopped. The propeller kept turning, but slowly now, in the wind, and everything was silent except for a whistling noise outside.

"Check your harness," Harold said again. He was adjusting levers, guiding the plane in from the sea, down, down. The tiny beach expanded and was now quite clear. They were aiming directly for the western end and Harold had the wheels down.

It was going to be all right.

Jordan realised that she had been holding her breath. She filled her lungs, easing the ache in her chest. Gliders landed safely all the time, and they didn't have engines. So what if Harold didn't like kids? He was a good pilot. He knew the beach was here. He knew he could land on it. He'd probably landed on it before. Heaps of times.

In the silent approach, they could have talked to each other, but they didn't. There was nothing to say. Baxter's grip on her hand was so tight, she thought he'd break her fingers. The red light pulsed like a heartbeat and above it, the yellow beach slowly unwound. The plane was close to the sea. Any moment the wheels must break the surface. But it wasn't water they touched. There was a bump and they bounced, up in the air, down again, bump, bump, running fast along crunching stones. Harold had his elbows out, working the controls. Still going fast. The beach was narrow, sea on one side, trees on the other, and they were halfway along it. The plane was slowing, slewing sideways in the gravel. Harold struggled and swore.

Near the end of the beach the left wing caught a tree. What happened then seemed like a film in slow motion. Jordan saw the plane make a deliberate turn and saunter toward a large old beech tree. Branches of the tree came to meet them, scattering leaves, twigs, glass, in a great shower.

The branches entered the cockpit right through to the backseat, and the plane stopped.

CHAPTER NINE

1 8 0 5

Hunter crouched in the grass, head lowered and turned toward Toru. The warrior's eyes were hard above his smile, and the axe in his hand was poised for that famous flick of the wrist. Hunter's unprotected back froze curved inward. He could almost feel the axe between his shoulder blades.

"The no-name is running to the pakeha camp," Toru said softly. "I knew it. Long ago, I saw the thought in your eyes."

Hunter said nothing. At least the axe would be a quick death.

But the axe did not come. The old warrior shifted it in his hand and said, "We have the moa."

Hunter briefly nodded and wondered at the delay. Perhaps Toru intended to torture him, after all. The flesh along his spine flinched with apprehension.

The warrior said, *"E tu!"*

Obediently, Hunter stood, his head bowed.

Then the warrior tucked the axe in his belt. "Go to the pakeha seal skinners. Today, I would not harm the bearer of Tane's voice. But watch where you walk, no-name. My sons will look for you, and when they find you, you will be killed."

The slave was so surprised that he looked directly into

the man's eyes, an offence in itself, punishable by death. But Toru merely waved his hand in an impatient gesture and turned away.

Hunter did not consider his bleeding hands and knees or the loose sealskin wrapping on his right foot. He turned and ran as fast as he could to outdistance the axe that might be thrown, should the old warrior change his mind. Through the tussock he went, across the stream, the foot wrapping flapping behind him. Only when he had run into the long shadows at the head of the valley did he stop and unbind his feet. He leaned against a cliff and drank icy water from a waterfall. He rubbed the blood off his knees with a handful of wet grass. Then he stretched his arms toward the sky and laughed.

He was free.

CHAPTER TEN

2 0 0 5

The darkness was full of noise and Jordan couldn't see. There were shrill noises, a siren voice echoing in her ears. Robbie's hands were on her shoulder, shaking her. "A cut, it's just a cut," he was saying.

She tried to open her eyes but saw nothing. There was wet stuff running down the side of her nose to her mouth. Tears, she thought, licking her lip. The salt was thick and had a strong iron taste.

"Your head's cut." Robbie shook her again.

She reached for him. "I can't see! I'm blind!"

"Wipe your eyes! It's just a cut. Baxter! Baxter, he's—"

"Baxter?" She groped with her right hand and felt wood. A tree branch. She remembered the slow swinging of the plane.

"There's blood in your eyes," Robbie yelled. "Jordan! Wipe your eyes!" He was doing it for her, rubbing her face, and she was seeing something through a blur. A tree. Leaves everywhere. Broken glass. Where was the noise coming from? An alarm? No. Baxter screaming, one breath after another. She tried to move and hit her head again. She could make out the broken end of a thin branch directly in front of her.

Robbie was rubbing blood off her face with her scarf. She put her hand out again and touched that thick lump of wood. Her heart jumped with fear. "Baxter? Baxie?"

"He's hurt," cried Robbie. "I can't reach him!"

Jordan felt for the clip on her harness. Her vision was misty and flickering, her hearing distorted. Baxter's screams and Robbie's shouting came to her ears in pulsing waves, as though she were underwater. She blinked, rubbed her eyes, and her hands turned red. She held her

62

fingers in front of her face and stared at them, then she looked at the wreckage around her. The branch at her right elbow was driven into the back of the seat between her and Baxter. It had just missed them. Above it were smaller branches, bent and broken, and leafy twigs. When she lifted them aside, she saw Baxter. The front seat had pushed back against him and another branch had come between him and the window. From this branch, a twig as thick as a pencil had speared his upper arm. The sleeve of his T-shirt was puckered around it, and bright red.

There were leaves everywhere, like green confetti.

"Baxie, it's all right! Shh! Shh! We'll get you out." She grabbed the front seat. "Harold? Harold, help us!"

The pilot didn't answer. His head had flopped forward.

Robbie was trying to see past Jordan. "Baxie, what's wrong?" he kept saying.

She said, "His arm's hurt. Can you open that door?" She unclipped Baxter's harness and mumbled, "You're okay, you're okay," although he wasn't okay, and they both knew it. She rubbed her eyes again. The blood was running down from her scalp and she guessed from Baxter's pop-eyed expression she must look a mess. "I'm okay, too," she said. "Shh! Can you stop that noise?"

He gave a great hiccup, closed his mouth, and the scream came through his nostrils as a high-pitched whimper. He was shaking all over.

Jordan wanted to pull the stick out of his arm, but she

didn't know how to do that without hurting him more. Her main concern was the pilot's seat pushed back almost to Baxter's knees. She wiped her eyes again. Where were Baxter's feet?

Robbie was leaning across the front passenger seat, trying to open the door. "It's stuck! I'll see if I can push it." He wriggled over the seat and landed facedown amongst twigs and broken glass. "I didn't get hurt at all," he said, struggling up, his back against the instrument panel. "The tree came in that side." He sat up in the front seat and parted the leaves to look at the pilot. His mouth opened and he went still. "Jordan, I think he's hurt. He's—" Robbie dropped the fistful of twigs.

Jordan slid across to Robbie's empty seat and, leaning down, tried to feel Baxter's feet. More blood filled her eyes and she wiped her scarf across her forehead. "Can you wriggle your toes, Baxie?" She looked at him. "Baxie, do you hear? Your feet, can you wriggle them?"

He nodded, whimpering.

Jordan wiped her face again. "You can really move them?"

Again, Baxter nodded.

"Robbie, Baxter can move his toes! You know what? Those crazy shoes! Those thick soles! They stopped the seat!" She reached down. "Baxie, I'm going to untie the laces, I want you to pull your feet out." She groped in the narrow space over one shoe, then the other. His legs were shaking like anything, his shinbones knocking

64

against her arm. "Lift your feet, Baxie. Do you think you can do that? Swing your legs toward me."

He cried out, his left hand waving at his right arm.

Jordan realised then that he would not be able to move until his arm was free.

Thump, thump. The aircraft shook. Robbie had his back to the branch between the seats, and was kicking the passenger door. Thump.

Baxter screamed.

"Robbie, stop!" Jordan cried. "The movement's hurting him." She knelt on the seat beside Baxter. "Baxie, remember Sherwood Forest? Will Scarlet had to pull the arrow out of Robin Hood's leg."

He stared at her.

"It hurt, but only for one second."

Baxter closed his eyes and screwed up his faced tighter than a washrag.

The branch was about the same thickness as an arrow. She didn't know how far it had gone into his arm, but at least it wasn't out the other side. She put both hands on it and felt a shudder go through him. "I'm going to do it now, Baxie. One, two, three!"

He yelled, but it came out easy, pulling out the red-soaked T-shirt. His arm was bleeding from a dark red wound, ringed with blue. She held up the stained, splintered twig so that he could see it. "About three centimetres, Baxie. The same as Robin Hood in the movie."

He stopped crying, but he still didn't talk. He shivered

like jelly, and now the plane was shivering with him. Robbie was back to kicking the door.

Jordan reached down and pulled Baxter's feet out of his shoes. He had a bruise under one knee but otherwise his legs worked, no broken bones. She reached through the branches and tapped the pilot on his neck, which was warm and rough like sandpaper. "Harold, you awake?"

"He isn't," said Robbie. "He's unconscious. I can't open this door, Jordan. I've tried and tried. It must be bent."

"Did you undo the lock?"

"What lock?"

"The lever under the handle."

"What lever under the—oh." Two clicks, a light push, and the door swung open. Robbie jumped out, turned, and reached for Baxter, who was able to climb over the seat by himself.

Jordan looked at the space behind their seat.

"Are you coming?" said Robbie.

"Our bags," she said. "I'd better get them."

But when she crawled over the seat into the luggage space, the plane made a groaning sound, rocked, and slid back about a metre. The branches pulled away from the backseat, creaking, scattering more leaves, and Harold's seat went forward. She could see Baxter's shoes.

"Jordan, get out!" Robbie yelled.

"Okay."

Their luggage had fallen to the back of the compartment, but she could reach the blue canvas satchel and Robbie's bag. She slung them over and followed them, climbing over the backseat and then the front seat. She passed the bags out to Robbie.

He dropped them and held out his hands to her. "Get out! Hurry! It's slipping into the sea!"

She turned toward the pilot and pulled away twigs. "Harold? You okay, Harold?" No. He was definitely not okay. Now she understood why his seat moved forward when the plane rolled back.

She wiped her eyes with her scarf. She'd assumed that a forked branch had come through the plane between the seats, missing them except for that twig in Baxter's arm. But that wasn't all. There was a third branch, higher and bigger. It was stuck through the middle of the pilot's chest. When the plane had slipped back, the tree had stayed stuck, pulling him, belted into his seat, against the instrument panel.

"Harold!"

He wasn't unconscious. He was dead.

CHAPTER ELEVEN

1 8 0 5

Hunter reached the next sound as the sun disappeared, and he decided not to push on to the seal skinners' camp. He was tired and hungry and there was time to spare. It would be at least two days before a search party was sent from the village. His evening meal was raw fish and fern roots; his bed a hasty gathering of moss and bracken fern, soft but damp, spread on rocky ground under a rimu tree. He untied the sealskin from his waist, lay down, and pulled the skin over his body. It, too, was damp, but that didn't bother him. The night was warm, and he was exhausted. Almost immediately he fell asleep.

His dreams were clear and without visions of moa or sky canoe. When he woke with the calls of kiwi in the valley, he felt that he was being dragged up from some deep, dark place of rest. The kiwi noise faded and he listened in the stillness to small sounds of water, a stream, the sea. There was no snoring, no barking of dogs, no crying children. He was alone.

He pushed aside the sealskin and sat up. For the first time in memory he was spending a night far from his captors and he felt strange, as though a large weight had been removed from his back. He looked through the dark tree to a clear starlit sky. The way of being a slave had gone, but he wasn't sure what was left. If the huhus refused him in their camp, what then? Where would he go? The village had long arms and every hand would hold a weapon.

He didn't know how old he was, fifteen or sixteen summers, and in his freedom he hoped one day to find a good *wahine,* a woman he could love and take to himself as the young men of the village embraced their wives. He wasn't sure what it would be like to love, but he had watched the village families, the mothers and fathers, their children, and their way of being. He had seen Te Hauwai's woman with a new infant at the breast while Te Hauwai chewed food and placed his mouth on the mouth of the older baby, feeding him with such tenderness that Hunter's breath hurt. That was what he wanted. To be a husband, to be a father, to work and hunt for his family, and to grow old with his woman at his side and grandchildren around him. That was the right way of being, and the way his heart leaned. He could endure aloneness when it was necessary, but it didn't suit him.

Sometimes he wished that he could remember his parents, if only to establish his *whakapapa,* the links with past generations. Many times he had tried with the eyes of his mind to see the man and the woman who had given him life, but any face that came to him was something he made up.

He pulled the sealskin around his shoulders and rested

his head on his knees. If he didn't have a past, then he would have a future. He would not be like the moa, the last of its kind, dying without making new life.

The sky was no longer clear in the morning. A thick mist covered the water and filled the spaces between the trees, greying the green of the bush, coating everything with fine water drops. The mist was a gift of Tane, for it meant he could light a fire and his smoke would not be detected. He set out to look for hardwood suitable for a fire stick, and when he found it, he scraped away the wet outer layer with his flint. Dry moss, shavings, bits of bark, scrub that would crackle like seal fat, leaves of mahoe to give a good sweet smoke, these he gathered. He would snare a bird, find some mussels, and he would eat an entire cooked meal himself instead of picking at bones and scraps left by others.

As he worked, he talked out loud. Long accustomed to whispers and silence, his voice was almost a stranger, and he enjoyed hearing it put sounds to his thoughts. He told the fire stick how he had found the moa, and he recited a chant of grief for the great bird that had been in his moe-mahi for many days. "Deep peace to you, brother moa. May your body feed the earth that fed you, and may you walk in freedom with your ancestors in the spirit land." He talked to the rimu tree that had sheltered him during the night, and wished it many seasons of growth. When he snared the wood pigeon, he sent its spirit on its way with a song of gratitude that continued as he packed wet clay around it. He set the clay ball on his fire and went to the rocky beach to gather small black mussels and water snails.

The mist moved around him and he thought of it as Papatuanuku's breath, the earth mother holding him close—as close as Te Hauwai held his child when he fed him. He stood tall and laughed. He liked it, this new freedom. Life in the village had not been good and he could never go back to it.

Again his thoughts went to the moa, and he wondered if Tane had sent it to free him from slavery. Then he considered Toru's kindness, a thing so unusual that he still could not believe it. His feelings grew too big for his thoughts, too big for words. He put the sealskin full of shellfish on the rock and, with a loud cry, leaped into the sea. The water was cold, as sharp as ice on his bare skin. He swam around in a wide circle, climbed back onto the rocks, and shook himself.

Through the mist he could see the disturbance he had made in the flat dark water, ripples that still travelled. He picked up his sealskin and slung it, weighted with mussels and *pupu*, over his shoulder. As he walked through the mist to his fire, the trees rippled like the sea and changed shape, and there in front of him was the moonlight girl with blood on her face. He stopped. Her image was blurred, but he could see all of her, and he thought she could not be a huhu, for her garments were not theirs. She was clad in the colours of flowers, petal skin covering her body, arms and legs in layers. Her feet had neither boots nor skin wrappings, but were enclosed with blue-and-white shells, and all of her, down to her feet, was splashed with the red that ran down her face.

She was a magic thing, he decided, come from the spirit world, and now she walked toward him, her hands outstretched, her eyes as empty as sky.

He felt two distinct movements within himself. He feared her because she could not be human, and his head told him that she had come to take him back to the spirit world. Yet his heart reached toward her, beating fast with concern, telling him that this Marama was wounded and needed him.

He dropped the bundle of shellfish and took two steps toward her to grasp her outstretched hands, but of course she was only a vision and she disappeared, leaving him standing with his hands held out to mist. Slowly he lowered his arms, his sense of freedom replaced by something much bigger. Many times in the last two days he had seen the waka, the white canoe, dropping out of the sky, and he knew it was the fall that had injured her. He also knew where to find her. She stood on the pebble beach where he had seen the waka sliding into the water, the bay of the dying moon, near the cave where he and the old men had sheltered from the storm.

She was asking for help.

He thought about this as he prepared his meal, and the significance of it overtook him with a feeling not sad, not happy, but heavy with responsibility. He peeled the baked clay from the pigeon. The feathers came off with the hot earth, leaving sweet, steaming meat. The mussels in the embers had opened. The sea snails were ready to be cracked. He needed food for strength, but the pleasure of eating it had gone.

He could not go on to the camp of the huhu seal skinners. He would have to return to the other side of the valley, to the cave where he had camped last night with the three old warriors. This was not what his head wanted. He would lose two days. A search party from the village would be sent out. The thought was like a fist around his stomach. But he had to go back. The girl's claim on his heart was too strong.

He put some pigeon flesh in his mouth and did not taste it. The risk of being caught would be very high. He swallowed and put his head in his hands, felt his hair, still wet from the sea. He would hurry. Perhaps he could answer his Marama's call for help and still be able to put a distance between himself and a slow, horrible death.

CHAPTER TWELVE

2 0 0 5

From the outside, the aircraft seemed barely damaged. The tip of the left wing looked crumpled and the front cockpit glass had splintered around a tree that leaned toward the sea. Jordan worked out what had happened. The small bay had a steep, narrow beach with trees close to the water. When the wing caught, the plane had spun around, impaling itself on the overhanging beech. If they'd stopped a few seconds earlier, it would have been a perfect landing.

She dragged the two bags up the steep slope and dropped them under a tree. Baxter was shivering and gulping and holding on to Robbie, who was trying to calm him. Jordan's scalp was still bleeding, although she could feel no pain. She looked at the plane, with its nose in the tree and tail in the water, and felt angry at the pilot for being dead. He was supposed to be looking after them. How could he have let this happen?

Sand flies hung in a cloud around her, landing on her face, her hands, feasting on her blood. They even flew up her nose. She slapped at them.

"What are we going to do?" said Robbie.

"We'll get help," she said, but she didn't know how. Her brothers looked at her, waiting. That was the trouble with being the oldest. Everyone expected her to have answers. For crying out loud! She didn't have half an answer! She didn't have anything! Her head hurt and they were lost somewhere deep in Fiordland.

The bay was in a narrow sound of dark water, walled with darker mountain ranges. Behind them a valley covered with dense bush led to yet more mountains. There were no houses, no boats, nothing moving but millions of sand flies.

Jordan put her hand to her face, then saw her scarf. "I'm going to wash the blood off." She took two steps toward the sea, and her legs folded so that she sat down hard on the stones. Now she, too, was shaking, suddenly as weak as a newborn kitten. She started to cry, but when she opened her mouth, sand flies flew in.

"Jordan?" Robbie sounded anxious.

She stopped the tears. "I just slipped." She crawled the rest of the way to the water's edge. The beach was so steep that she needed to anchor herself in the small sharp stones to keep from sliding in. She could see the bottom to about a metre from the shore, but after that it dropped away to blackness. She scooped up water to wipe her face and hands. It was icy cold. About now, she thought, their parents would be at Invercargill Airport, waiting for them.

She was rinsing the blood from her scarf when a screeching noise made her jump. It came from the plane. She turned, eager with hope. Harold wasn't dead, after all!

He was alive and getting out to help them. It was what she wanted to believe, even though she'd seen the branch in his chest. "Harold!" she yelled.

"It's not Harold," Robbie said.

No, it wasn't Harold. Glass and metal had screamed on branches as the plane slid back a little way, the tail settling lower in the water. She stood on legs that felt like jelly, and wobbled toward Robbie and Baxter, holding out the dripping scarf. The sand flies followed her. "It's a bandage for your arm," she told Baxter. "My beautiful new scarf."

The boys were in black clouds of sand flies. Robbie was trying to keep them off Baxter, who was gulping and sobbing. Robbie said, "How are we going to get help?"

"Search and Rescue." She shook the wet scarf. "They'll send out a helicopter. Hold up your arm, Baxie."

"They don't know we're here. No one knows we're here." Robbie lifted his brother's arm by the hand so that she could wind the scarf around the wound. "It's just mountains and trees and sea."

"They'll find out. Stink! They can trace planes, you know."

"How?" Robbie insisted.

"They've got instruments, little black boxes and beacons and things." She tried to smile at Baxter. "We'll get rescued tomorrow. Tonight we'll have a camp under the trees. How does that feel on your arm?"

Baxter stopped crying long enough to say, "It's wet."

"Of course it's wet. I had to wash it. You wouldn't want my blood mixed up with yours, would you? Be thankful, Baxie. You know how much this scarf cost?"

Robbie was breathing fast. "No one'll rescue us. We'll die."

"Shut up, Robbie!" She paused to brush the flies away from her nose. "Look! We're okay, aren't we? If we were meant to die, we'd have—" She looked at the Cessna and the branch stuck through the dark shape in the cockpit.

Robbie gave a small hiccup. "You've still got blood on your face. Your hair's an awful mess."

She tucked in the end of the bandage and pulled down Baxter's red-stained sleeve. He was still shivering. "I know."

"I'll bathe it for you, if you like," Robbie offered.

"Later," she said. "I'm going back in the plane."

"No!" Robbie grabbed her jacket. "It could slide into the sea."

Jordan paused. The Cessna was parked at a steep angle, its tail now in the water, but it was their only hope of some comfort. There might be food in there, some blankets, tools. Maybe distress flares. Did planes carry those? She looked at the dark mountains that propped up a sagging tent of cloud. It was going to rain. "I won't go back in the luggage space. I'll just look around the cabin. Harold had a cigarette lighter. We can make a fire."

Robbie's forehead was scrunched into lines. "If it starts to move—"

"I'll jump out fast," she said.

She walked through weeds and stones to the Cessna, which sat like a big dead bird washed up by the tide, a crumpled wing smeared with mud and grass. She reached for the open passenger door and a shock ran through her. It was as though she had touched a live wire, yet it didn't come from electricity. It was the name again, *Marama*, shouted in her head. *Marama! Marama!* The echo was a current through her body, a vibration in her arms and legs.

It was the voice she knew and yet didn't know, the same voice that had sounded the words *waka* and *Marama* in her sleep. She stopped, her arms still tingling, and looked at the door. Then she turned and trudged back to Robbie and Baxter. "It's too late. I'll do it in the morning. We'll find some big stones to stop the wheels from rolling back. I'll get the other bags and the cigarette lighter. There's sure to be a first-aid kit on board with ointment, you know, insect repellent, other stuff." She talked fast to fill the silence around her. "They'll rescue us tomorrow. They'll see the plane."

Finding a place to camp was not easy. Under the mat of weeds, the ground was damp, stony, lumped with bits of dead trees. The best place was in a grove of rimu near a small stream, a short distance from the beach. Jordan and Robbie cleared away rocks and fallen branches and tried to cover the ground with a thin mattress of ferns and leaves, but the earth was still hard. The knots of tree roots came through, and everything they touched felt damp. Eventually, they sat between ridges of roots, their backs against wet bark.

"My arm's sore," whined Baxter. "I'm cold. It's nearly night and I'm hungry."

Jordan swallowed a lump of tears. "All right! All right!"

She opened the bags and handed out Robbie's clothes. She took the dressing gown because it was the biggest, and put a thick sweater on Baxter, leaving one sleeve empty. Robbie pulled a woollen hat over his head to protect his ears from sand flies. Then he shared his spare socks. Good old Robbie, thought Jordan. Who cared if his socks always ponged? They were thick enough to keep off the insects.

She undid the blue canvas bag that contained Aunt Allie's presents, although it was supposed to stay closed until Christmas Day. They knew what two of the parcels were, a Christmas cake for Mum and a Swiss Army knife for Dad. They opened the cake tin first, pulled bits off, and stuffed it in their mouths. It had been a long time since the snack at Christchurch Airport. Even Robbie, who didn't like fruitcake, licked his fingers. They used the pocket knife to cut Jordan's apple, and they drank from her water bottle, which she refilled at the stream.

It was almost dark when Jordan unwrapped the other

presents. Baxter had a kaleidoscope, Robbie had a book about the pyramids of Egypt, and Jordan's parcel contained a T-shirt which appeared to be red. "No inflatable mattress!" She tried to laugh. "Oh, well, two out of five isn't bad."

"What'll we eat tomorrow?" Robbie said.

"We've still got half the cake."

"That won't last long."

"We'll find food."

"Right." Robbie shrugged. "We'll throw a stone at a wild deer."

"There's a packet of dried apricots in my bag. I'll get it in the morning. We'll find the cigarette lighter. We'll make a fire. There's probably something in the plane we can use for a shelter. You know, like plastic cover."

"He's dead," said Robbie. "Harold's dead."

Jordan took a long, even breath and wiped her forehead. Sometimes you saw dead people on the TV news, and they looked dead. But Harold's face had looked as though he were sleeping, eyes almost closed, bushy ginger mustache hanging over mouth and chin. It seemed he was just in a peaceful nap, except he wasn't breathing and there was the branch, and his shirt and jeans shining with red—She curled her fists. "Stink! We need that stuff out of the plane. My hipsters are in there, my blue tank top, the Celtic ring Grandma gave me. All my gear!"

Baxter began to cry again. "You said we'd get rescued tomorrow."

"Or the next day," Jordan said, closing her eyes. She had a headache and she was tired of trying to sound cheerful. They were in the middle of a wilderness and no one knew if they were alive or dead. By now it would be on the TV news. Mum and Dad would be falling apart. All their children on a small plane that had crashed. Where? They wouldn't know where because the pilot had changed their course. Jordan bit her fingernail. Well, serves them right, she thought in a wash of anger. Harold had asked if she had a cell phone. No, she didn't have a cell phone. But she'd begged and pleaded for one. Dad kept saying no, she was too young, and anyway, those things could give you brain tumours.

She imagined herself here on the beach, unfolding her phone and pressing numbers. "Hi. Is that you, Mum? It's Jordan here, calling from Fiordland. There's been a plane crash. The pilot was killed, but we're okay. Could you please tell Search and Rescue to send a chopper? Oh, and Mum, we had to eat your Christmas cake."

It wasn't funny. None of it was funny. The sand flies left as the light disappeared, but the bites remained and itched like crazy. She could hear the stream gurgling, and somewhere in the forest, birds screeched at one another. Beyond that, there was nothing except silence.

She arranged the almost-empty bags on the ground. Baxter would have the blue one for a pillow. She and Robbie would share the other. She felt the cut above her forehead. It was wet but not bleeding, and it scarcely hurt, although her head still ached. She thought that maybe scalps didn't have too many nerve ends, or something like that. She lay down, trying to fit her body around lumps in the ground. Robbie put his head beside hers and said in her ear, "They'll be at Invercargill Airport."

"And Aunt Allie will be at Auckland Airport—on her way to America," she said. "So what?"

"They'll know," said Robbie. "About the crash, I mean. But they won't know we're alive."

Baxter was whimpering. "My arm is sore. Jordan? My arm is hurting."

Jordan turned up the collar of her jacket. She loved her brothers, but right now she wanted to yell, Shut up, shut up, what do you expect me to do?

"Everything'll be better tomorrow," she said. "Go to sleep."

CHAPTER THIRTEEN

1 8 0 5

Hunter ran all morning. The sun sucked the mist from the earth, leaving the air bright and clear and the leaves shining with newness. In this place where rain fell four days out of five, an entirely clear sky was a rare thing, and the birds sang of it, their calls echoing across the valley. Hunter felt the sun on his head and shoulders and the earth warm under his feet. But as he ran, he regretted having discarded his foot wraps, for although the soles of his feet were hard as the bark of a tree, the rocks were even harder and he was collecting cuts, and splinters from thorn bushes.

In the tussock land there were signs of the moa, but now the presence of the bird in him had gone, and when he ran past a claw print or scratch hole, no sight or smell came to him. The moa was dead, and in a few days of rain, the holes and prints would be filled, all traces removed from the earth. In the village, Te Hauwai would have his cloak and perhaps the head and feet. The body would be too tough for a fire, but it might be slow-cooked in an earth oven, if the old warriors had the strength to carry it back to the village without their slave.

He wondered where the men were. They would not waste time, lest the moa skin spoil, and Te Hauwai would be in a hurry to send young warriors after the runaway boy. That would be their thinking. Probably they had spent the night in the cave and this morning marched along the shore, already heading toward the village. Of one thing Hunter was sure. The men had not encountered the three spirit children. They were still beside the beach. Hunter saw them there in his moe-mahi, the girl, the two boys, a vision that had come to him several times. In the first seeing, Marama knelt by the sea, washing the blood from her face. Later, as he was running through the tussock, he saw again, the waka rolling back over the stones, into the water, with the girl trapped inside. He stopped and called her, so loud that her name echoed across the valley. *"Marama."* His voice froze the air, pushing back the sunset, scattering birds from the trees. *"Marama."* The vision broke before him like a bubble of foam, and once more his heart rested in his body, certain that she was safe. "I'm coming," he told the girl. "I am coming as fast as my feet can tread earth."

Later, and less distinctly, he saw the three children huddled under a rimu tree, asleep, and he believed they were not spirit children at all. No creatures from the other worlds needed sleep. Not ghosts, not fairies. They were as he had first thought, huhu children, but of a different kind than the seal skinners. They bled. They ate and drank. The black flies bit them. They slept as all people of flesh and bone sleep. But he didn't understand why they had come in a magic waka, so light it could fly, so heavy it could sink. Nor did he know why his heart was connected to them, especially the girl, in this way.

Some time in the afternoon, he entered the forest where he had last seen Chief Te Hauwai. Here, the usual birdsong was smothered by the drone of big bush flies. They were everywhere, black swarms speeding through the trees. He followed them and found the place where the warriors had butchered the moa. They had taken the legs and head as well as the skin, but of the flesh they'd carried off only the breast. The remains lay under a tree and were crawling with the black flies, intent on laying eggs.

He paused. It was a way of being that all creatures were devoured by other creatures, and their energy passed on. The moa became a fly, the fly became a bird, the bird became a man, and in the change, all gave something of themselves back to Papatuanuku, the good mother earth. It was right, then, for the flies to have what was left of the moa, but it would be better for the moa if it were given directly to Papatuanuku. He found digging tools, a stick, flat stones, and worked for a long time to make a hole big enough in the rocky soil. The flies buzzed louder at being disturbed as he dragged the shapeless carcass into the hole. As he covered it with dirt and stones, he again sang his song of gratitude for the place of this moa in his life.

He wiped his hands. The sun was going down. He needed to get to the beach before nightfall to protect the children from further harm. The cave was known to many people as a place of shelter. His visions told him that the three old warriors had not found the children. But the danger was not over. There could be other warriors in the area. Soon a crowd of young men would be hunting for a runaway slave. He needed to find the huhu children and take them to the huhu camp before they were all killed.

He ran out of the forest and through the wider part of the valley, where flax and tussock made long shadows and the wood hens called to one another along the crease of the stream. He was tired and ready to eat, but he kept running until he was at the cave. He stopped in the entrance, his body bent, hands on thighs, his chest heaving to draw breath. The cave's shadows were empty and the fire ash cold. He straightened, turned, and ran to the beach.

The crescent of brown stones was bare of life, as were the trees that grew along it. Nor was there any mark on the beach to show where the waka had been.

The children were not there.

CHAPTER FOURTEEN

2 0 0 5

They did not sleep well. The hard ground stiffened their bodies, putting aches in their dreams. They lay close to one another, and when one moved, the others woke up. Baxter cried when someone bumped his arm. Robbie talked in his sleep. It was a long night.

Jordan thought she hadn't slept enough to dream, but when Robbie called her, she was far away and someone was with her. She opened her eyes to grey mist, grey lichen hanging from grey branches above her head. She heard Robbie's voice, high-pitched. "Jordan! Jordan, wake up!" She propped herself on her elbow, and her matted hair pulled at her scalp. This morning the cut was definitely sore.

"Jordan!" He was standing between two trees, flapping his hands at her. "The plane's gone."

"Huh?" With her mind still blurred by sleep, she thought he meant that Harold had flown away to get help.

"The plane, the plane!" Robbie was jumping up and down. "It's gone."

She stood up and rubbed her back. Baxter was still sleeping, his good arm under his head. "What do you mean, gone?" she said.

"Come and see."

She stumbled over tree roots and down to the water's edge. The tide was in, washing up as far as the grass, and the sea was littered with bits of bark, twigs, and leaves. The broken tree hung out over the water. On the splintered end of the main branch, there was a dark red stain as thick as paint. Already it was moving with flies.

But there was no aircraft.

Jordan clenched and unclenched her hands. "Gone," she said.

Robbie whispered, "What about Harold?"

She remembered how she had been stopped from climbing into the cockpit, and a coldness crawled along her spine.

"Harold was in there!" Robbie shouted.

"I was nearly in there!" she yelled back.

"We should have gotten him out." Robbie's eyes filled. "He might have only been unconscious."

"Stink, Robbie, he was dead. You saw he was dead. I saw him, too. He wasn't breathing." She slapped the sand flies that swarmed around her nose and mouth. "Oh, Robbie, my bag's gone down. All my things! At least you've got your clothes."

Robbie blinked and tears fell onto his cheeks. "People can look like they're not breathing and just be unconscious. Now he's drowned."

"Robbie! He was dead! You ever see anyone with a tree through their middle, not dead?" She shut her mouth. As usual, she had carried the conversation too far. She took a couple of steps toward the tree and was stopped by the blood on the big branch. Robbie saw it, too, and he was crying quietly, his shoulders jerky. She wanted to put her arm around him, but she couldn't. She was too angry with the plane, the tree, the pilot, with everything. "No cigarette lighter. We're freezing and we can't even make a fire."

He rubbed his eyes and didn't answer.

"How's anyone going to find us if we don't have a fire?" She looked around at the empty sound. Everything was a shade of grey—sky, hills, water—and there were sand flies everywhere. "Planes have first-aid kits and flares." The anger fell away to a deep despair. She put her hand on the back of Robbie's neck. "He didn't drown, Robbie," she said. "He was buried at sea."

But Robbie could not stop crying. "He might have a wife and some kids wait—waiting for—him."

They went back to their sleeping place and found Baxter crying. Robbie took his slippers from the black bag and put them on Baxie's feet. Jordan unwound her scarf from his arm. The beautiful silk was truly ruined.

Baxter's arm was painful, swollen and red around the wound, and he complained that every movement hurt it. She washed the scarf, this time in the little stream that trickled into the bay, and again wound it around his arm. Then they sat under the tree to eat half of the remaining Christmas cake. It was sweet, sticky with figs and raisins, and they ate slowly with small bites. Jordan wanted more. Robbie, too. But no one said anything. The last piece in the tin looked very small.

Jordan rubbed her hands on her jeans to warm herself. She thought of the cigarette lighter under the sea and slapped her knees. "Stink! We need a fire."

"I think we should sit out on the beach," said Robbie. "If a plane comes over, it'll see us."

"It's going to rain," she said.

"How do you know?"

She jerked her head toward the sky and felt pain in her scalp. "That front coming through."

"We'll get just as wet under the trees," Robbie replied.

For a while they sat in silence and Jordan tried to remember where she had been when Robbie woke her. Someone had been walking beside her, telling her something. It wasn't a voice so much as a kind of knowing, as though the person with her had deliberately placed a picture in her head of a cave in the trees. It was a dream, of course, but sometimes dreams were about real things. She wondered if she should tell Robbie about it, thought, No, no, don't be silly, then, Yes, why not?

"I reckon," she said, "there's a cave over there."

"A what?" said Robbie.

"A cave."

"How do you know?"

"It's a—you know, a sort of premonition."

"Like you were sure we'd get to Invercargill."

"I didn't say that."

"Yes, you did!"

"That wasn't a hunch, Baxie. I was just trying to cheer you up. This is different. A cave, a shelter—over there, past those trees."

"Search and Rescue won't see us in a cave," insisted Robbie.

"They won't see us in this mist." She spread her arms. "Mist is cloud, Robbie. Cloud down to sea level, and it's going to rain heaps."

"How do you know it won't clear?"

"Because that was the forecast. Heavy rain. Are you going to sit on the beach in the rain?"

"My arm's sore!" wailed Baxter.

"We have to find shelter." She stood, wincing at the stiffness in her back. "We're supposed to go in that direction." She pointed toward the trees. "I know. I—I just know."

Robbie's face was stubborn. "A hunch isn't shelter."

"There's no harm in looking, is there?" She saw Baxie's face pinched with pain. "You two stay put."

"You'll get lost," warned Robbie.

She looked into the misty gloom. There was no sense of north, south, east, or west. Getting lost was a distinct possibility. "We'll call each other. I'll keep yelling your names, and you keep yelling mine. One yell every five seconds. I promise I won't go any farther than your voices."

Robbie looked at her, his eyes full of doubt. "Your hair's still a mess. I said I'd wash it for you."

"When I come back," she said, walking away from them.

She entered a forest so thick and dark, it could have been under the ground. Tall trees swallowed up most of the light: rimu, beech, mahoe, and five-finger. Beneath them grew tree ferns and small shrubs, then wet moss and tiny ferns in a bog that squished up the sides of her shoes.

"Robbie?"

"Jordan!"

Mist filled all the spaces of air like grey smoke so that it was difficult to see more than an arm's length in front of her. Banners of pale lichen hung from branches to drip against her face. Cobwebs beaded with moisture laced the joints of branches. Everything was wet. Everything smelled of clay and rotting wood.

"Robbie? Can you hear me, Robbie? Baxter?"

"Jordan! Jordan!"

She tried to remember where she'd been in the dream and who had been with her. A cave. Somewhere. The trees looked the same whichever way she looked, black ogres in the mist, and she was no longer sure of anything.

"Robbie? Baxter?"

"Jordan."

Their voices were closer, which meant she'd been moving in a circle. She stopped and called again. "Baxter?"

"Jordan."

They were like birds singing to one another. Baxter was a fantail, Robbie a bellbird. What was she? She didn't know. Maybe a *tui*. Tuis sang a lot, but sometimes they hit sour notes.

As she swung her leg over a moss-covered log, she noticed a change in ground level. She no longer walked in a swamp but on small plants set in solid earth, and to her left, a bluff loomed out of the mist. It was as tall as a house, had big stones lying around and some trees growing on it.

"Baxter?"

"Jordan?"

"Robbie?"

"Jordan."

Beyond the stones, the bluff had an overhang, much

like a porch roof, while underneath was a hollow with a smooth earth floor.

"Jordan?"

It was so near the beach that she could see dark water through the mist and trees.

"Jordan?" Robbie's voice was shrill with concern.

"I've found it!" Recognition turned in her like a key in a lock. This was the place of her dream. "Robbie? Baxter? I've found the cave."

CHAPTER FIFTEEN

1 8 0 5

Hunter slept in the cave that night. In the morning he looked for the children in the forest and along the beach. They were close. In his moemahi, he felt their distress, the pain of the small boy's wound, the other boy's fear. His head picked up the ache in the girl's skull, but that was less now and would heal. They were all hungry. They were all tired and frightened. So where were they? The girl had called to him for help and he was here to give it, but now it seemed they were hiding from him.

Wait for me at the cave, he'd told the girl. Did she not understand?

Time was running out. He would have to leave soon

if he were to avoid the slave hunters. He stood on the beach stones, looking at the mountains wrapped in mist, the flat water. Two seabirds flew against their reflections. Farther out, a seal surfaced, waved a flipper, and dived, leaving rings of silver ripples. How could he tell the moon girl and children that he needed to take them to the seal skinner's camp, to their own people? Again he called, his voice hanging in echoes across the water. *"Marama! Tamariki! Haere mai, haere mai!"* Marama! Children! Come, come!

He thought he might coax them out of hiding by preparing a meal for them. He risked lighting a small fire on the beach, and he placed near the flames some cod, shellfish, a few freshwater crayfish, a leaf basket of wood grubs, and another of ripe tree fuchsia berries. He left it, and when he came back later, the food was untouched, the fire burned down to ashes.

In his moe-mahi their presence was very strong. How could he not find them?

Hunter had learned years ago that his gift could not be commanded, it was given and often unexpectedly. He had no control over his visions, which were sometimes clear and sometimes as vague as dreams, but when he saw a bird hiding in reeds, the bird was there. When his seeing showed him an eel in a hole in the riverbank, he could put in his hand and take that eel. He did not doubt, then, that when he saw children on the beach, there would be children on the beach. But in truth, they were nowhere to be seen with his outer eye. This disturbed him. There were also changes in the land he could not explain. The sky waka had fallen into a tree on the beach, yet there was no such tree. The mountains and the sea were the same shape, but there were small differences. A rock slide on the face of a mountain in front of him was covered with forest when he saw the children in his vision.

He searched all morning in a mist that became light rain. He went back to the cave, and as he walked through the trees, he saw them. The air shimmered, spreading like water, and in the ripples the children appeared, all three resting in the cave. So she was here! They were waiting for him!

But when he parted the branches, he found the cave empty. In the shadows was the dead ash from his cooking fire. Beside it lay the coil of his fishing line. That was all. He stopped, closed his eyes, and in the space behind his eyelids, he saw the children clearly. They were here, but they were not here.

Truly, Marama had found the cave. It was in the same place, but it was so different that Hunter hardly recognized it. The ledges had gone and the recess had no depth. A *ponga* tree fern grew in front of Marama's cave, and there were trees above it instead of bare rock.

Hunter looked into his deep, empty cave. He closed his eyes again. At once, its image shivered and changed. It became shallow, surrounded by new vegetation, and in it were the girl and the two boys, who were surely her brothers. The vision passed. He opened his eyes and his cave was once again itself, deep and empty. He squatted on the shadowed floor to think what this could mean.

There were two worlds, he decided, two lands separate but alike, resting beside each other like two villages. Hunter was in one. The children were in the other. The connection between them was strong because they were in the same place. That was why he had been able to prevent Marama from getting into the waka and most surely drowning. His warning had taken great energy from him. Afterward, he had trembled like a dying fish. It was much easier to touch the moon girl's thoughts and guide her to the cave. Even now he could close his eyes, whisper, "Marama," and see her head turn to search the cave in her world. She didn't see him, but she heard him.

Hunter wondered if the dangers in her world were the same as in his. Warriors might not find the children, but they still needed help. The girl and her brothers were hungry and their pale skins were covered in black-fly bites that itched and would turn into sores. The older boy was unharmed. Marama had a head wound, almost healed. The small boy, though, the hole in his arm was filled with putrid matter that would increase through his entire body until he died.

Hunter went to a flax bush by the stream and asked Tane, god of the forest, if he could cut some leaves. With his flint he removed some of the long, glossy blades from the outside of the bush and carried them back to the cave.

He split the base of the stem, squeezing the clear, sticky sap onto his arm. He squeezed more on his arm, more on his hand. "Marama, Marama," he chanted. "Marama, *titiro mai*." Marama, look at this. But his concentration was disturbed by the thought that the three old warriors would now be at the village and, without doubt, a party of young men with justice in their mouths and blood sport on their minds would be heading his way.

Hunter shivered as with cold. He did not dare think what they would do to him.

CHAPTER SIXTEEN

2 0 0 5

Robbie sat near the entrance of the cave, holding out his hand to show a struggling sand fly. "It works! They don't like it. If they land, they get stuck in the goo."

Jordan scraped some of the jelly from the base of a flax stalk and spread it on her arms. She folded the pocket knife. "This has got a lot of blades, even a little saw. Robbie, we could split these leaves to make a flax fishing line. That's what people did in the old days."

Robbie was smearing the sticky flax jelly over Baxter's cheeks.

"Don't get it in his eyes," Jordan warned.

"How'd you know this was insect repellent?" Robbie asked.

She scratched some dried blood away from her hairline. She was hungrier than she'd ever been in her whole life. "I don't know. I think I read it somewhere." She picked up the longest flax leaf. "We've got to catch some food. If we cut thin strips of this, and braid them, we could join them to make a line. I've got safety pins for hooks."

Baxter frowned. "How do we cook fish?"

She shook her head. "Sashimi."

"What's that?" asked Baxter.

"Like sushi. You know. Japanese."

"Yuck," he said.

Jordan glanced at him. He looked sick. His face was still flushed, his eyes puffy, and there were red sand-fly lumps on his forehead. The sticky flax sap looked like snot on his cheeks. Maybe he'd be better when they found something to eat. All the fruitcake was gone. They had nothing left, zero, big fat zilch, and the emptiness in Jordan's stomach was a nagging pain. Last night she had seen mussels on some rocks, but that was at low tide. They'd have to wait hours to get some.

"My arm aches like anything," Baxter said. "It's hot."

"We'll wash it again," said Jordan. She was worried because he'd grown quiet, this noisy little brother, Baxter the clown, Baxter, who put whoopee cushions on a visitor's chair, and plastic poo on the toilet seat. He lay back, his head on Robbie's bag, while she unwound the bandage. Every time she touched his arm, however lightly, he winced.

At the stream, she rinsed out the empty cake tin and filled it with water for washing. She put the scarf, now a stained rag, in the current with a stone on top to hold it. Clear water ran over it and through it, loosening small brown clouds of blood.

She went back to the cave and used one end of the wet bandage to bathe the wound that was now a crater in a mound of red skin, swollen, hard, hot to touch. He cried when she washed it, although the icy coldness of the water gave him some relief.

The cloud had thickened and a fine mist of rain drifted over the trees. Robbie slit the long blades of flax into strips as thin as string. He ran the strips over the back of a pocket knife blade to soften them, and Jordan braided them, threading in new strips as she went. It took ages to get a length of line. They talked about the blue canvas satchel and the presents they would have liked from Aunt Allie.

Robbie said, "Pepperoni pizza. Bananas. A fishing line and some hooks. Toilet paper. A rope, a tent, a box of matches."

"Doughnuts," said Baxter. "Chocolates. Ointment for my arm."

"Nachos with cheese." Robbie held his stomach. "A double chicken burger with fries and a strawberry milk shake."

Jordan listened to the rain hissing through the trees. "A cell phone," she said.

They were quiet then. Jordan thought of their parents getting the news for Christmas. She had decided she wouldn't mention the awful things, like Harold, like Mum and Dad learning the plane was missing, but the thoughts kept coming back. She twisted the thin strips of flax between her fingers. "You know, I hated that book about the Swiss Family Robinson. When they got wrecked, they found everything they needed. Stink! I mean everything! They even had animals and—and sugar!"

"We've got a kaleidoscope and a book about the pyramids," said Robbie. "But it's not all useless stuff. There's a really good pocket knife and a cake tin. My bag, Jordan. That's useful. Clothes. Two safety pins."

"Robinson isn't even a Swiss name," said Jordan, braiding a new flax strip into the line. "They kept finding all this stuff washed up on the—" She stopped and looked at Robbie.

"Beach?" said Robbie.

"Was the plane door open or closed?" She tried to remember.

"The front glass was almost gone," said Robbie. "Things could have floated out. Maybe our bags, the cigarette lighter, clothes." His eyes grew wider. "Do you think Harold—"

For a second she imagined the pilot floating facedown in the sea like a log, then she said, "No, his harness was done up. Hey! The cigarette lighter was plastic. Maybe it—" Her shoulders dropped. "No. It'd get full of water."

Robbie glanced at Baxter. "We might find the first-aid kit."

When they had finished the fishing line, they tied an open safety pin to the end and, farther up, slipped a long, narrow stone through the braided cord. They gave Baxter the kaleidoscope and Jordan's watch and told him they would be back in an hour.

"We're going fishing," Jordan said.

Robbie nodded and ran the coiled line through his hands. "The tide's in, Baxie. Could be something washed up from the plane."

There was a whisper of wetness on the trees and a few drips from leaves to earth. In the open, the rain was heavy enough to wet them in seconds, but as Jordan said, it was an easy way to have a wash. The dark water was ringed with rain, drops bouncing in circles. Farther out, a curtain of heavier rain billowed between them and the other side of the sound. The hills, wrapped in shreds of mist, were dark grey and already marked with the white threads of waterfalls.

Jordan's bare feet arched over wet grass and pebbles,

sending her messages of rough and smooth, slippery, hard. Her toes curled on dead leaves. Walking with bare feet, she decided, was another way of seeing.

The tide was up, covering the beach, but they were able to walk through the grass to the tree with broken branches, the one Robbie called the killer tree. Leaves and twigs floated near the shore, but there was nothing from the plane.

"Look out there!" cried Robbie, standing on his toes and pointing.

She thought he'd spotted something, but it was only a small oil slick making a rainbow on the water.

Jordan shook her head. "Stink! Stink! Nothing!"

"Gone-burger!" said Robbie in a mournful voice.

They agreed they would not fish in the bay, not with the plane down there. Jordan had strong feelings about that and Robbie didn't ask questions. They took their line to the rocks at the far end. They would try fishing from the other side.

The tide was still too high for shellfish bait, but Jordan pulled up some clumps of grass and uncovered three pink earthworms and some short white grubs that curled up in the palm of her hand. "Huhu grubs," she said. "You know, if we got really, really hungry, we could eat these."

Robbie didn't answer.

"I reckon I could," she told him, bringing the huhu grubs almost to her mouth. But she didn't. She couldn't.

At the end of the bay, they did find some things from

the aircraft, but nothing of use. Robbie picked up a soggy clipboard that had most of its paper washed away. He dropped it again. One of Baxter's platform shoes was lying on the stones—only one. Farther on, amongst more leaves and twigs, bobbed something of a light colour. They thought it might be some kind of jellyfish or a fishing float. Jordan picked up a long stick and dragged it into the shore. When they saw what it was, they started to laugh, and their laughter grew until they forgot their hunger and held on to each other, breathless.

"Swiss Family Robinson!" Jordan gasped.

It was a watertight plastic bag containing two stained sick bags with Robbie's digested steak pie.

There was no beach in the next bay. Steep slopes came down to the water's edge, and the stunted trees that grew on them had roots spread over rock faces. Linking the two bays was an outcrop of rock, and on this they sat in the rain and uncoiled their fishing line.

Jordan had never fished this way, but there was in her a knowing. Had it come from the voice? She wasn't sure. Flax. Flax jelly. Flax line. These things had been familiar although she had never used them before. Not the safety-pin hook. That was Robbie's suggestion. The idea of a bone hook had come into her head. Bone hook, bone hook. But Robbie said the safety pin was sharper and anyway, until they caught a fish, where would they find a bone?

"I'm starving!" he said.

It was a long time before they caught the first fish. Their thick flax line wanted to float and they had to find a bigger stone to weight it. Then, when they did get a jerking bite, the fish flattened the safety pin and took the worm. The safety pin had a tendency to open out wide, and they left it like that, bending the pin side to make a hook. It worked. The next time they tried, they caught a small greyish-brown cod that flapped on the rock beside them. Without hesitation, Jordan put her fingers in its gills, picked it up, and brought it to her mouth. She bit it hard on the top of its head and it went limp.

Robbie stared at her. "Why'd you do that?"

"To kill it."

"Yuck! Couldn't you have hit it with a rock?"

Jordan didn't answer. She didn't know why she had put the fish's head between her teeth. She'd done it quickly, without thinking.

Robbie's face was puckered with distaste. "Biting a live fish!"

"It isn't alive now." She put it, soft and shining, into the tin, and breathed hard. How did she know to bite the back of its head? She'd never killed anything before. Nothing. Yet her teeth remembered the feel of it, as though she'd done it many times. She ran her finger over the sandpaper roughness of the cod's scales. Never mind. She was too hungry to feel sorry for it.

Robbie rebaited the hook.

"We could always make a fire by rubbing sticks together," she said.

Robbie sighed. "Have you ever tried rubbing two sticks?"

"No."

"I have. It doesn't work."

"It works on TV."

He fed the line carefully over the rock, into the water. "You have to have special woods, one soft and one hard, and you have to do it flat-out for hours." He gasped and jerked the line. "Got another one!"

"Okay," she said. "We eat at a Japanese restaurant. Sashimi, Robbie. Fresh sashimi."

Robbie pulled in the fish, big this time, and a dark blue-green colour. It thrashed against the wet rocks, flicking them with salt water. "Quick! Don't let it get away."

Again, she did it. Fingers into the gills; fish lifted wriggling to her mouth, one quick crunch behind the eyes. A shiver went through the cod and it hung from her hand as limp as a wet sock in her hand.

Robbie looked in the opposite direction. "Baxie won't like sashimi."

Baxie! She looked at her bare wrist, forgetting that her watch, which she left with Baxie, no longer worked. How long had they been here? They had to get back. She jumped up and hurriedly coiled the flax line between her hand and elbow.

"He's real sick, isn't he?" said Robbie.

"It's just a sore arm. You take the fish. I'll bring the line."

Rain trickled from Robbie's hair into his eyes. He blinked and more drops ran down his nose. "No," he said. "It isn't just a sore arm. Jordan, it's worse."

CHAPTER SEVENTEEN

1 8 0 5

It was a way of being that when water contained a dead body, the place became *tapu,* or sacred, and no one could take fish from that water for at least six months. Hunter had managed to guide the girl away from the bay to a rock fall at the beginning of the next inlet. She was quick to learn, this Marama, and the fishing line, though thick and clumsy, was strong and the right length, once she had attached a heavier stone.

To see her and her brother pull up the cod gave Hunter a warmth in his heart and eyes. He remembered Te Hauwai with his son of less than two summers on his lap, thought of the softness in the chief's face as he chewed meat and passed it on, his mouth on the baby's, like a parent bird. It was as though Te Hauwai was chewing a part of the sun that lit his face and sharing it with his child.

Hunter knew that feeling as his own as he watched

Marama and the boy on the rock, and he laughed at their surprise and pleasure to pull in a large fish.

Their world was so close to his that he could see them every time he closed his eyes and often when his eyes were wide open. Marama's image was strongest, although he was sure she didn't see him. She seemed not to notice his presence, even when he stood face-to-face showing her how to plait flax for a fishing cord, but a part of her thinking would absorb what he was doing and sometimes she would frown as though she were wondering where an idea had come from.

Hunter had forgotten to eat, there being no space for food in the feelings that filled him. Not only did he feel responsible for Marama and the boys, but a sense of possession had come upon him. He did not want them to belong to a spirit world. He wanted to see them with outer seeing, to touch the girl's white hair, put a poultice on the younger boy's arm. He wanted them to see him, too, so that they could go with him to the seal skinners' camp. In time, Marama would be his woman, and the boys his brothers. They would sail far away with the seal skinners, and be a family. That was what the warmth of his heart told him. But there were other feelings, sensations of great dread that crawled the length of his back as he thought of the many feet drumming the earth, coming closer, closer.

He could not wait in this place much longer. Before he left, there was the medicine she had to make for the younger boy.

"Marama!" he called. "Marama!" He left the cave to find a *kawakawa* tree. "Marama!" There was one by the stream not far from the cave, but would it be so in her world? He pulled off small, heart-shaped leaves and some shoots, held them up. "Marama! Titiro mai!" Look!

Back in the cave, he squatted on the ground and filled his mouth with leaves. He chewed, his eyes closed, seeing her face close to his. Her hair was soaked with rain and the cut above her hairline was visible, almost as long as his thumb. "Marama!" The first lot of chewed leaves he spat on the ground. His mouth was now prepared for the making of the poultice, and he filled it full of the kawakawa. As he chewed, he took the flint from the cord at his waist. He could not demonstrate with his upper arm, where the boy was injured. It had to be between his wrist and elbow. Carefully, he spat the pulped kawakawa onto a blade of flax and laid that across his lap. Then, with the flint, he cut into his flesh.

"Marama!" he instructed. "Titiro mai!" Watch! He put the arm to his mouth and sucked, drawing in his cheeks, tasting the sea and land flavour of his own blood. He kept sucking, although the cut was not deep and the blood had ceased to flow. It was important for her to understand that she could not stop too soon. He spat, put his mouth back to the cut, spat again. Finally, he put the poultice against the cut and bound the flax leaf around his arm. This is for your brother, he tried to explain. If you do not do this, he will die.

The effort of holding the connection had tired him and he walked from the cave stiff-legged, like an old man. There was no more time. He would have to leave this place or he, too, would cease to live.

CHAPTER EIGHTEEN

2 0 0 5

The rain was no longer light. It dropped with needle points they could feel through their sodden clothes as they walked back to the cave. Acupuncture, thought Jordan. But they weren't as cold as they'd been this morning. The rain seemed to bring a change to warmer weather.

Baxie was asleep in the cave, his head on the blue bag, his face red and flaking with dried flax sap. They let him sleep and went out again, this time to the stream, where they cleaned the fish in the fast-flowing water. Rain pounded their backs, their heads, and ran in their eyes. It would wash the blood out of her hair, Jordan told Robbie.

The blades on the Swiss Army knife were as sharp as razors and it wasn't difficult to cut the cod into small pieces. The flesh looked good, glassy white with small rainbows in it, and they ate bits during the cutting.

"It really is like Japanese sashimi, Robbie. Actually, better!"

They kept the tails and bony bits for bait, arranging the rest on the big plastic bag that Robbie had emptied and washed.

Robbie shook water off his hair. "You were right. It's that southeasterly front. It finally came over the mountains."

"At least we've got some shelter," she said. "A cave is a lot better than a tent."

"Better than sitting on the beach," he admitted. He looked at the sky, his eyes narrowed against the rain. "No plane'll ever find us in this. We're stuck until the rain clears."

"They won't send a plane. It'll be a chopper. Stink, Robbie, those eggbeaters can fly under really low cloud."

"If they know where we are."

Jordan scratched at a sand-fly bite. The rain had washed off the jelly. She would need to cut more flax leaves. "I told you, they'll track us. All planes have got beacons that send out signals." She looked at him. "Even under the sea."

He wasn't so sure. "We should put a flag on the beach."

"A flag!" She stared at him. "Good idea! I'll donate my Christmas present from Aunt Allie—my new red Cool Babe T-shirt."

"We could put it on—" He looked at her. "On that tree."

Her hand dropped. They walked through the wet grass, their shoes creaking with water. Red flag on a bloodred tree. But no, she thought, the rain would wash the tree as it had already washed her hair. By the time he put the shirt up, it would no longer be a murder weapon, just an old broken branch.

They sloshed through the bush, the swamp water now ankle deep and cold. Jordan straddled the mossy log. "A flag's okay, but a cell phone would've been a lot easier."

Baxter didn't want any fish. He was in a grumpy mood because they'd left him on his own. "It isn't even a real kaleidoscope!" he said, throwing his Christmas present with his good arm. "It hasn't got anything in it. And your watch is busted."

"Look! Food!" cried Robbie. "Delicious sashimi. We caught it ourselves."

Jordan picked up the kaleidoscope. She saw what Baxie meant. It was one of those mirror-scopes that multiplied whatever image came into view. She held it to her eye and saw a lot of tiny Baxters, then a multitude of tree roots on the cave ceiling. She turned it over to study the lens. It was fat and round. "Hey! A magnifying glass! We can make a fire!"

"How?" said Robbie.

"We've got paper. We can take the glass out of this thing and focus the sun on the paper until it burns. Cooked fish! Cooked mussels! Dry clothes! A bonfire on the beach to let the world know where we are!"

Robbie sighed. "It won't work."

"It will! Look at it!"

Robbie pointed to the cave entrance dripping with rain. "No sun," he said. "You're right, Jordan. A cell phone would be easier."

Baxter refused to eat. Jordan and Robbie finished the big fish between them, and put the rest in the cake tin.

"You'll like it later, Baxie," Jordan said. "When you're feeling better."

"I hate raw fish."

"You can pretend it's buttered popcorn. Holy guacamole! Look at all that rain!"

"I hate rain!" He turned his head away and she realised that although his face was hot, he was shivering. He was very sick and she didn't know what to do. Her helplessness turned to an anger that reached out, groping, to blame someone—Harold, Aunt Allie, the airlines, her parents, God. Why couldn't they have found a first-aid kit washed up from the plane? One lousy little first-aid kit. Was that too much to ask?

Robbie was tying one end of the fishing line to a Ushaped tree root on the ceiling of the cave. "Clothesline!" he said. "We can tie the other end to that tree fern and dry our clothes." In his pajamas and sandals, he ran out in the rain to fasten the flax line, but it wasn't level. It sloped down toward the tree fern and their clothes ended up as a clump of wet washing outside the cave.

"Another failed experiment," Jordan said.

Robbie turned. "Yeah, right! Everyone knows you've got all the smart ideas."

"I didn't say that. I don't have—" She closed her mouth, seeing him close to tears. It wasn't true. Some of the ideas weren't even hers. She didn't know where they came from. "I need to change Baxie's bandage," she said.

As the day went on, the rain grew heavier. Drops were falling down the cave entrance like a bead curtain, and even the small, hairy roots that hung over their heads had moisture on them. They could hear water moving the stones in the stream.

They sat in silence. Jordan steered her mind away from awful things and remembered wet weekends, mornings when they all got into their parents' bed and Dad brought them hot chocolate and toast. One wet Saturday afternoon, Dad had spread a sheet of plastic on the living room floor and brought in the lawn mower to fix it. The three children had helped. When it was put together again, Baxie had turned the starter key. The mower roared and jittered about, chewing up the plastic and the carpet underneath. Mum was as wild as a bear with a sore head. "Not an ounce of sense amongst the four of you!" she'd yelled. But afterward she was kind of proud of the carpet with the haircut. When visitors came, she'd lift the rug that covered it and show it off as a big joke.

Marama!

She jumped. That voice again! It had sounded loud in her head, causing that same electric tingling.

Robbie, who was sitting near the cave entrance, looked up. "What's the matter?"

"Did you hear anything?"

He listened. "Rain," he said.

"I mean, feel. You know, a feeling. Do you suddenly get shivery like—like this cave is haunted?"

"A ghost?" He looked around the cave. "Oh, please!"

"I keep hearing someone, Robbie." She paused. "A voice calling my middle name."

His eyes widened. "A ghost! You mean—Harold?"

"No! No, not Harold! Someone else. Why my middle name?"

"Jordan Marama McKenzie."

"No, not the Jordan McKenzie bit. Just Marama. I'll tell you who it sounds like. You know Hohepa Ropiha?"

"The guy you're in love with?"

"I am not!" She felt her face get hot. "I don't even like him all that much!"

"Not half," said Robbie.

She wished that she hadn't mentioned it. Hohepa was their head prefect and captain of the school's A soccer team. The only person who knew how she felt about him was her friend Cathie, and even Cathie hadn't been told everything. Jordan glared at Robbie. "Will you listen? I'm serious. This voice keeps calling my name."

Robbie scratched in the dirt with a small stick. "Maybe you're getting like Cousin Andrea."

She thought about that. Dad's cousin Andrea had an illness and had to take pills to stop her head from hearing voices. "Maybe," she said, wondering if Robbie could be right. After all, her whole body was made up of genes inherited from her ancestors, and she guessed that some of Cousin Andrea's genes were there right along with everyone else's. She scratched at a sand-fly bite. She'd read somewhere that even personality was inherited in the DNA. Wow! If Aunt Allie studied geneology, she might stop going on about being a self-made woman.

Robbie was still looking at her. "Does it happen all the time?"

She shook her head and changed the subject. "Why don't you read your pyramid book? Read it out loud to Baxie. Baxie? You want to hear about pyramids?"

Baxter lay against the bag, his face red and shining. "No! I'm thirsty!" he cried. "I hate this cave! Jordan, I'm hot! My arm hurts."

"I just filled your water bottle."

"I drank it. I want more."

Jordan shrugged off Robbie's dressing gown and went out in her underclothes, skin bare to the drops that fell as big as hailstones. Back home she wouldn't even go into the kitchen like this, but here it didn't matter, and they couldn't afford to get any more clothing wet, or they'd all end up sick. She took her plastic drink bottle to the stream that had grown quickly into a fast-flowing river, and squatted at the edge. Although she filled the bottle from surface water, there was still a bit of fine sediment in it, but at least it was cold. The bottle felt like an ice pack in her hand.

On the way back, her feet took her on a meandering path to the patch of trees behind the cave, and there she stopped under the dripping branches, sounds of water all about her. To the left was a small bush of dark green heart-shaped leaves, glossy with wetness. She pulled a leaf off and put it in her mouth, tasted it, then spat. She shook her head. Why had she done that? The bush could well be poisonous. She spat again and went back to the cave with the water bottle. Baxter, she thought. Baxter has a bad fever.

CHAPTER NINETEEN

1 8 0 5

Hunter could not leave the bay. He had failed to communicate the healing to Marama and he would have to try again; otherwise the boy would be dead within days. Yet it was too dangerous to remain in the cave. The warriors would come here first. He cleared away all signs of his presence with a branch of a *manuka* brush, sweeping the floor of prints, making sure that the fire he'd lit on the beach that morning had been erased by the tide.

He would not go far. The next inlet had no beach. The rock was steep, almost unclimbable, but he would go the long way around, taking some of the plant with him, and climb to the top of the cliff, where he would see any movement below. There was no vision of the warriors in his moe-mahi, but he could sense their feet beating the earth at a running pace. It was likely that they would merely glance at the cave and run on across the valley, over the slope and into the other sound. But when they reached the camp of the huhu seal skinners and found that he was not there, they would double back and start a careful search.

That morning he had removed thorns from his feet, but there were cuts that had opened to sores, and he knew that his pursuers would have sealskin wrappings. Nor did he have a weapon. They would have clubs, axes, and spears. There was one of him, there would be twenty or thirty of them.

It was almost dark by the time he had worked his way to the top of the peak, and he couldn't see much for the mist that had come in, thick and cold. He sat in the steep incline between two rock faces and felt the weakness in his legs. He still had not eaten and his stomach groaned with hunger. He leaned against the cold rock wall, took the branches of heart-shaped kawakawa leaves from the cord at his waist, and closed his eyes.

Marama. Marama. The seeing began almost immediately, the girl lying in the cave in a loose garment, her hair over her face, her eyes closed. The sick boy lay nearby, breathing fast in fever. The older boy, like the girl, slept. *Marama.* He breathed her name as he chewed the leaves, spat, chewed again, the bitterness curling his tongue. This time, he spat onto a whole kawakawa leaf. Now he picked up his flint, held it between thumb and forefinger and opened the cut on his arm. He sucked at the blood. He was tired and losing concentration. He didn't want to do this. He didn't even know if he could enter the girl's sleep. *Marama. Titiro mai! Look at this!*

The warriors arrived.

The mist around him was as thick as a wall. Through it he heard the crunching of beach stones far below, and the shouting of many voices. A war party. They had come with the sunset, running along the water's edge, but they wouldn't look for him tonight. It was the cave they were seeking, shelter, food, and rest before the morning man-hunt. Hunter listened into the mist and nodded in satis-faction. The warriors would not find the children. The cave in the forest below was not the cave of the children's world.

Marama. Titiro mai. He sucked the blood from his arm, then he picked up the leaf poultice. *Look, Marama!* He bound it on his arm with a strip of flax. *This is what you must do for the boy,* he told her. *Do you under-stand? Like me, you are running out of time. Do this! Do this now!*

He closed his eyes, saw her frown and sigh in her sleep. In spite of his pleading, she did not wake up.

In his own world, voices continued to rise through the mist, jokes shouted, bursts of laughter from the cave. Hunter drew his sealskin around him and crouched lower between the rocks. I am like the moa, he thought. I, too, am the last of my kind.

CHAPTER TWENTY

2 0 0 5

On the third day, Jordan woke with a splash of water in her ear. Her body felt cold and water, dropping from a tree root on the dirt ceiling, splashed the back of her head, her neck. She turned over, moving her head. Another grey morning, heavy with rain. Inside the curtain of rain at the entrance of their cave, the earth seemed mostly dry. It was hard to tell in the poor light. She stretched and felt an ache in her spine. A warm smell enclosed her, as though the falling water at the entrance was an airtight door, a smell like bad meat and burned feathers. She sat up. Baxter's head had rolled off the bag. He lay near her, eyes almost closed, his face so hot that when she reached for him, it was like putting her hand near a fire. The smell was partly his breath and partly because he had peed his pants.

"Baxter?" She put her fingers on his cheek, his mouth, and felt his lips, dry and flaky. "Baxie, do you want some water?"

He whimpered but didn't answer.

He was very ill. The knowing of it went through her with a terrible certainty. Yesterday it had been just a sore arm and she had been thinking how lucky they were to get out of the plane without horrible hurt. If it hadn't been for Baxter's big platform shoes, his feet would have been crushed. They would never have gotten him out and he would have drowned. She could have drowned. Stink, they could have all been killed. That's what she'd been thinking. All day yesterday, she'd been preoccupied with stupid things like not having a cell phone, losing her bag, getting their clothes dried, and being hungry. That was the worst thing. Hunger. Feeling sick with emptiness. She'd even gotten mad with Baxter for complaining. Sore arm? So what! She had a bump on her head, she'd told him.

But Baxter's wound wasn't as simple as Robin Hood's Hollywood arrow. It had an infection in it that was making him burn with fever. People could die from this. The poison spread right through them, septic—septi—something, and their hearts stopped. She'd read about that in a war book.

Baxie might die and there was no one to help.

"Baxie, wake up! Do you want a drink?"

His breath came out as a long, foul-smelling moan, but he didn't answer. She propped his head on her leg and put her the water bottle in his mouth. He sucked at it, so she knew he wasn't unconscious.

How long before that happened?

She watched the bubbles go through the water bottle as he drank. If only they'd found the first-aid kit from the aircraft. If only— She didn't finish the thought. Last night, she and Robbie had promised not to say *if only*.

She wiped water away from the corner of his mouth. His lips were cracked, his eyes puffed up like bee stings. First-aid kit, she said to herself. Leaf poultice. She went still with remembering. Who had told her about the leaf poultice? Was it Mum, or Dad's sister Ripeka? Did she read about it somewhere? She had stopped by that plant yesterday, and she hadn't known why. But there was more, wasn't there? She thought of the pocket knife and the rest came back to her. The voice! That's how she knew!

"Robbie," she said. "Robbie, wake up!"

She went to the stream in her underclothes and came back, her pale hair and skin dripping. "It's like a river," she said, putting down the cake tin full of water and the plastic bag containing the washed bandage. Nothing was sterile, she thought, nothing absolutely clean. The tin had contained cake and fish, the plastic had held a bag of Robbie's vomit. She had done her best to wash and rewash them, but the roaring stream was probably full of bugs anyway.

"You're cold," Robbie said to her.

"I'm all right."

"No, you're not. You're covered in goose pimples."

"I'll warm myself on Baxter, won't I, Baxie?" She pushed back her wet hair and felt the bump and cut on her head. It was still a little tender, but it hadn't become infected. "I have to go out and get the leaves now," she told Robbie.

"Are you sure you know the right ones?"

"Yep." She nodded and her hair fell back over her face. She was sure. The knowing had set firm in her head. Now it buzzed and raced with urgency. "I have to hurry."

Robbie had a cautious look. "Maybe Hohepa Ropiha told you," he said slowly.

Jordan knew what he was getting at. "No Cousin Andrea, Robbie. This is real." She opened the pocket knife, looked again at Baxter, and then ran into the rain to find the bush.

Don't die, Baxie, she prayed as she ran. You can't die. You're my brother.

His upper arm was like a swollen sausage, hard and hot, the skin shining red with darker streaks down the inside of the arm, although the actual wound seemed to have grown smaller, a tight-lipped mouth, ringed with blue. He moaned when Jordan propped his arm up on the canvas bag, but he didn't make too much fuss. Under the wounded area, she laid the only clean bit of clothing left— Robbie's green underpants with the black and white music notes. The black bag was under Baxter's head.

Robbie knelt by Baxter and held his other hand, but Baxie wasn't taking too much notice of anything, except to whimper when they moved him. His eyes were closed, his breathing fast.

Jordan breathed a Maori prayer. *"E te Atua awhina mai ki ahau raua ko Baxter."* O God, help me and Baxter.

She laid the washed scarf on top of the plastic bag and stuffed her mouth with leaves. They were bitter and made her tongue curl, but she chewed and chewed until they were mush and there was juice dribbling down her chin.

Then she stood, walked to the entrance of the cave, and spat.

"What'd you do that for?" Robbie said.

She didn't know, could only tell him, "It's the way it's done."

She sat down and filled her mouth again, wet, slippery leaves that broke between her teeth, releasing juices that made her stomach rise. Yes, this is the way it was done. When the mixture had pulped, she leaned over the plastic bag and spat a mound of green stuff onto the bandage. But there was still the knife. She had already washed the small blade, but it had been used for cleaning fish and there would be bacteria, all kinds of stuff on it. It meant more leaves, more chewing. She spat the third lot onto the plastic bag, wiped the knife blade through it several times, and dried the blade on the end of the bandage.

Robbie, who was still holding Baxter's hand, was blinking as though she was going to stick the knife into him. "This is the worst bit," he said.

"No," she replied. "Not the worst bit."

She had been quick in pulling the twig from Baxter's arm. This was even faster, the knife poised for a breath-holding moment, and then a quick in and out. Baxter had not seen it coming, but he certainly felt it. He screamed and his body arched. He threw himself away from her and the stinking stuff from his arm dribbled over Robbie. The blood looked black and there were yellow streaks and watery stuff in it. Robbie's face twisted.

"Don't puke!" Jordan warned as she put the knife down. "Look away!"

The arm kept dribbling. When Baxter recovered from the fright and pain, he let her mop up the stuff with Robbie's green underpants. His screaming had dropped to a high-pitched moaning and his chest heaved, reminding Jordan of a frightened bird.

"It pongs," Robbie said, his head turned away.

"Hold him!" Jordan said. "This is the worst bit!"

"What are you going to do?"

"What people do for snakebites," she said. She saw his look of horror and added, "If you're going to throw up, do it outside."

She took Baxter's hot hand in hers and leaned over his flushed, damp face. "This won't hurt you," she promised. "Keep still. I'm going to kiss it and make it better." She felt her tongue against the roof of her mouth, rough with the astringent juices of the plant, as she came near the weeping wound.

E te Atua awhina mai, she prayed. Help me, help me.

CHAPTER TWENTY-ONE

1 8 0 5

Hunter closed his eyes. He could not go yet. It was not finished. The girl had come to it late, and she would need to draw the wound again and again, applying fresh poultices each time. If he departed now, he could lose contact with her.

He had not slept well. The rocky crevice had been like a bed of axes and the cold mist had invaded his sealskin, chilling his bones. He felt some comfort in his heart that the girl had followed his instructions, but he was weak with hunger and the soles of his feet, normally as tough as tree bark, had cut like split fruit. These bare feet would not carry him far over the mountains.

He had not yet solved all the mysteries of the white waka and the children. Every explanation he tried had answered some of his questions, but not others. He was sure they had come from a land that was an echo of his own. Mountains and sea were almost identical. They reflected each other. He did not know how these strange huhus lived in their world, nor why they were so important to him, especially the girl with her sky eyes and white foam hair. No other visions had so enslaved his heart. He sat in the mountain crevice, knees drawn up, the sealskin draped around him, watching the sun thin the mist. Grey rags of moisture tore, and through the holes he saw the dark water and a flock of white birds wheeling in a food dance. There was no sound yet from the cave. The young warriors would still be asleep.

He knew all the young warriors down there. He had grown up alongside them. Some had taunted him. Others had not been unkind. Now they were fired with pleasure at the thought of hunting the hunter. He could expect no mercy.

As the sun came through the mist, he took off the seal-skin and laid it across his knees. With his flint, he cut it in half. If he were to escape, he would need new foot wrappings.

The mountains on the other side of the valley were forbidding, grey slopes too steep for trees, with tops always white with snow. It was over these, not through the valley, that he must make his way to the seal skinners' camp.

Briefly he closed his eyes and saw the sick child lying in the cave, asleep. The other two were in the rain, kneeling over their fishing rock, gathering mussels and kelp.

There was now a stirring of voices below Hunter. The warriors were awake and talking amongst themselves in the subdued way of men with sleep in their mouths. When they had filled their bellies and departed along the valley, Hunter would climb down the slope, make thongs for his feet wrappings. Then he, too, would eat in preparation for his journey across the mountains.

Someone shouted. Hunter jumped. There was more

noise, and a warrior called, "He is wounded! He has not gone far!"

They had discovered the broken kawakawa bush by the stream.

CHAPTER TWENTY-TWO

2 0 0 5

Baxter was sleeping, his face still red, hair stuck flat against his scalp. A flake of dry skin on his lower lip fluttered with each breath. Sometimes his eyes roamed about under their thin blue-veined lids. Sometimes he moaned.

Jordan wiped his face with a wet shirt. His skin was still hot, but the swelling in his arm had gone down. Blood and pus stained the bandage. Soon she would need to do it all again, open the wound, suck it, put on another poultice of chewed leaves.

"That stuff might make him worse," Robbie said.

"It won't." She rinsed the sock in the tin of water and washed Baxie's forehead. "I know."

"You get wrong hunches."

"No, I don't."

"You do. You do." He folded his arms across his stomach.

"Get some more mussels," she said.

"I can't. Tide's too far in."

Her own stomach was aching with hunger all the way into her throat. She carefully lifted Baxter's head onto the softest part of the bag. "My hunches aren't wrong. Sometimes I read wrong messages into them. But this isn't a hunch, Robbie. I told you. This is real."

Robbie didn't answer, but his eyes said a lot, big eyes, the dark shadows under them giving him a ghost face. He picked up the water bottle and went out.

Jordan stuffed her mouth with the medicine leaves and began to chew. Yes, she often got hunches. How she interpreted them could be wrong, but the feelings themselves were never wrong. In Wellington, for example. When she saw the plane. Stink! She'd gone freezing cold with dread, even though she'd tried to talk herself out of it later.

She spat the first lot of leaves and refilled her mouth. The voice had nothing to do with hunches. It called her, telling her what to do. The knowing was strong, like a memory.

She lifted Baxter's arm a little and began to unwind the bandage.

Her friend Cathie believed in guardian angels. Maybe that's what it was, a guardian angel putting advice into her head. It had stopped her from climbing back in the plane. It told her what to do to Baxter's arm.

"Baxie?"

He moaned and his eyelids fluttered.

"Baxie, I know you hate being kissed."

His eyes opened wide and he tried to pull his arm away.

"It's okay! No knife this time! Just a kiss."

He trembled, but he let her unwind the last of the bandage and lift the poultice. The chewed stuff was a funny colour and stuck to the wound, which was open and dribbling.

"I'm thirsty," Baxter moaned.

"Robbie's gone to the stream to fill the water bottle," she said, but she knew it was not altogether true. Robbie had gone out to the stream to have a good cry.

At low tide, they went to the beach to gather kelp and mussels. Robbie was red-eyed and cranky. As she cut the slippery brown seaweed, he called, "Don't drop that knife. It's Dad's Christmas present."

"I won't."

He wrenched little black mussels off the rocks. "What are these called in Maori?"

"Kuku," she said.

He put the mussels in the pouch of his T-shirt. "I'd rather eat mussels than seaweed."

She brushed wet hair from her eyes. She was tired of rain, tired of being hungry. Just plain tired. "Baxie's getting better."

Robbie raised his head so that his chin was pointing at her. "You can't go around eating bits of stupid old seaweed."

"It's kelp. It's good for you. People take kelp tablets."

"People make kelp tablets," said Robbie. "They do things to the seaweed—like cooking and drying it."

Jordan folded the knife. "Did you hear me? Baxter's arm. It's better."

"I heard you." Robbie bunched the mussels in his wet T-shirt. He was choking on a throatful of tears.

She was too tired to comfort him. "It was those leaves. I told you they'd work."

He made a croaking sound. "I'm going back." He turned and ran, the mussels rattling like stones in a pouch.

Jordan put the knife in the pocket of her wet jeans. They didn't have much to show for two hours of food gathering, a small cod, some kelp, a bunch of mussels, Robbie in a sad mood. It was hunger, she thought. Hunger and rain were a terrible combination.

What were Mum and Dad having for lunch? Or were they on the phone, in front of the TV, talking to the police, too sick at heart to think of their stomachs?

She carried the cod, which had paled in death, and the long strands of kelp over the rocks and along their beach. The rain beat down as though it were trying to make holes in her skin. Stink! she thought. Big stink to the Swiss Family Robinson and all those movies that showed glamorous people on deserted islands. You never saw swarms of sand flies and big black bush flies that laid eggs on your clothing. They didn't tell you that when your skin was wet, the dust turned to mud on it, and your hair got so matted, you couldn't even comb it with your fingers. Even the books that said you could use leaves for toilet paper were wrong. Had any of the writers seen the size of these leaves?

She wondered if Maori tribes had lived in this place before the Europeans came to New Zealand. She doubted it. The only creatures that thrived here were flies, big and small.

Baxter turned his head away and closed his eyes, but she kept the fish in front of him. "You have to eat!"

"No. It isn't cooked!"

"Cod sushi. It's good for you."

"I hate it!"

"You've eaten it in Japanese restaurants."

"That's different fish!" He rocked his head from side to side, his mouth screwed up into tight refusal.

Jordan put the piece of cod wrapped in kelp leaf in her own mouth. It really did taste good. She picked up another. "Baxie, you haven't eaten for days. You won't get better if you don't eat."

"Just leave him alone," said Robbie. "Can't you see he's not hungry?"

She was about to protest at the unfairness of the remark when she saw that Robbie had melted into tears. Poor Robbie. He sat near the entrance of the cave, his breath heaving with sobs. She put her arms around him and realised that he was still shivering. He rested his head on her and bawled against her shoulder while she patted his back. She could feel his shoulder blade, sharp as a garden trowel. His wet hair smelled like sour butter. She said the only thing she could think of. "It does taste good, Robbie. It really does."

Baxter went back to sleep and the rain, which had sounded like drums all morning, lightened to a drizzle. Robbie ate some of the kelp and fish, although he kept sniffing and wiping his nose with the back of his hand.

Jordan passed him some raw mussel. "Think of it as a hamburger and fries," she said. "Double-thick strawberry milk shake."

He gave a hiccuping laugh and shook his head.

"Rain's easing," she told him.

He rubbed his face. "Too cloudy to find us."

She scrubbed his hair with her hand, then stood up. "I have to get leaves for Baxter's arm. A new poultice every four hours."

"Does it—" His mouth curled up into that *m* shape and he couldn't finish.

She shrugged. "Just a metallic taste. It has to be done." She unfolded the pocket knife. "You don't have to watch, Robbie. You can read your pyramid book."

"Yeah. Suppose." Robbie crawled across the cave and unzipped the end pocket of his bag. "Aunt Allie asked me what I liked and I said dogs or basketball. Why'd she buy me something about pyramids?"

"How would I know?" Jordan briefly closed her eyes.

"Stink, Robbie! You expect me to have the answer to everything!"

He put his head down quickly but didn't cry. He sat cross-legged in his clay-smeared pajamas and laid the book on his lap. He wiped his hand on his jacket before he turned a page.

Jordan sat beside Baxter, her hands over her eyes. Rain, hunger, sore head, and itchy bites came together in the form of one huge tiredness that made her arms and legs shake. She was sick of being the eldest! She wanted to curl up on the cave floor and have someone look after her for a change.

Robbie had his back to the cave entrance. He was bent, his face almost on the paper, and was reading aloud. "One of the greatest mysteries of all time—" He stopped, looked up. "What's that?"

Jordan heard it, too. A bush fly in the cave. But bigger, farther away, a droning louder than the sounds of water.

It was a plane flying overhead.

The book landed in the dirt and they almost collided in their rush out of the cave, through the bush, branches in their faces, down to the beach. They waved their arms and shouted at the empty grey sky. The plane was on the other side of the clouds. Its bumblebee buzz faded, quiet, quieter, until they heard nothing but the whisper of rain around them.

Their arms dropped. They walked back to the cave, the

last of their dry clothes no longer dry, Robbie swallowing, his throat going up and down, his eyes glassy.

"It'll be fine tomorrow," Jordan said. "Sun for the kaleidoscope glass."

He nodded.

"They'll be back, Robbie." She put her arm around him, shaking him gently. "We'll light a fire on the beach and you can put up your red flag, my new Cool Babe T-shirt." She pulled his head against hers in a rough hug. "Until then you can wear it. You're wet as a frog."

CHAPTER TWENTY-THREE

1 8 0 5

The warriors knew the healing power of the kawakawa plant, and finding the stripped bush, they had assumed that the no-name was injured. From his hiding place above the beach, Hunter heard the excitement in their voices, even though many of their words were lost in the mist. He knew that they would divide, small groups spreading out in all directions, and before long some of the men would climb these slopes and find him. He could not stay any longer.

Quickly, he unwound the fishing cord from his waist, cut it in half, and used it to tie the pieces of sealskin around his feet. Then, bare but for his foot coverings, he moved along the top of the slope, from one rocky outcrop to another. For now, he had the mist to keep him covered, but soon the sun would devour every last grey shred of moisture and the men would see him moving like an insect on a wall.

He was no longer sure how he would cross the mountains. How could he get across the valley to those peaks? The hunters would be everywhere in twos and threes, eyes sharp for signs. A broken twig, a turned stone. These things would betray him. His only advantage was their belief that he was injured and with a fever. They would expect him to be weak, unable to move far or fast.

These rocky cliffs showed the hard side of Papatuanuku, the earth mother, and in them, he felt her lack of forgiveness of her sons who had separated her from sky father Rangi. True, the mist she wore around her bones protected Hunter from his enemies, but it also prevented him from seeing where he was going. He looked for a way down to the scrub line, where he could find cover and then slip into the sea, his only hope. He could swim like a dolphin, crossing most of the sound underwater, and because they would be looking for an injured slave on the land, they might not see him.

He wished he had eaten last night. His legs shook with the fatigue of hunger as he placed his feet sideways on the slope, steadying himself against rocks and small bushes. Through gaps in the mist, he saw the water far beneath him and he knew that if he slipped, he would bounce from rock to rock before his body splashed into the sea. As he moved, he listened, trying to gauge the distance between him and the voices that came up from the valley. How sure they were of finding him. He heard their laughter. One even called him by an unclean name to let him know that he would be carried back to the village in small pieces. At that, the others had yelled with triumph, like children playing games of war. The sounds echoed around back and forth in the mist as though every tree had turned into a jeering warrior.

Hunter paused on the side of the cliff and closed his eyes for a moment, but in his moe-mahi, he did not see the men. Marama and the older boy were on the beach of their world, tying something to a tree. It looked like a cloak the colour of *rata* blossom. They flickered and disappeared and he saw the small child sleeping in his fever.

I am the moa, Hunter thought. I have waited too long in this place and now I am trapped. But I will not finish on the end of their spears. I would rather drown or die the cold white death on the mountaintops.

He put his left foot against a small bush and brought his right foot down beside it. The sealskins protected his feet but made him clumsy. The bush came loose, and the stones around it. He swung across to another foothold as the plant and pebbles fell, gathering increase. He couldn't see through the mist, but he heard the noise as it swelled into a roar of rocks tumbling down the slope. Then there was a long splashing sound.

That noise was not as threatening as the silence that followed. He listened but did not hear a single word. They'd all heard the rock fall and now they had a direction. They would find him.

CHAPTER TWENTY-FOUR

1 8 0 5

Baxter had slept most of the day and by nightfall was wide-awake, wanting to talk. He asked about the plane. Had they seen it? Could they tell from the engine noise how big it was? Would it come back?

Although there'd been no evening meal, the hunger cramps in Jordan's stomach had gone. She felt weak and light-headed, trembling at the edge of laughter. The plane. That big blowfly plane. Someone knew they were here. What was the name of that finder thing? Emergency locator beacon, Robbie told her. All aircraft had them. It would work even if a plane was underwater. Was he sure about that? Nearly sure.

They talked until the cave was so dark, they couldn't

see one another. They breathed in the smells of wet clay, wet clothes, wet bush, and breathed out memories of home.

"Secrets," said Jordan. "Let's tell secrets. Robbie, what's something you never told anyone?"

Robbie's voice was warm. "When I was five, we visited Mr. Zimmerman, and I didn't know where the toilet was. I peed in Mr. Zimmerman's rubber boot on the back porch."

Baxie laughed at that, a croaky noise that sounded like crying.

Jordan told them about the time she and their cousin Dylan had tried tongue kissing. "We were eleven," she said. "The kids at school said it was dead sexy to kiss with tongues in each other's mouths."

"You didn't!" said Robbie. "Not that stupid Dylan!"

"We didn't know how. I opened my mouth and put my tongue out. He did the same. Then we closed in. It was like a sword fight."

"Was it sexy?" Baxter asked in his croaky voice.

"No! It was horrible." She rolled over to face the cave entrance. It was quiet out there, the only sound, the stream washing stones, and so dark, she couldn't tell where the cave finished and the trees began. A stillness came over her. Suppose the plane hadn't been looking for them? Suppose it was just an ordinary flight a bit off course?

"Baxie's turn," said Robbie.

There was a small squirmy noise, then Baxter said, "I read Jordan's diary."

"You didn't!" Jordan sat up. "What did you read?"

"Boring stuff."

"What kind of boring stuff?"

"About how you like Hohepa Ropiha but he's got another girlfriend."

"Stink, Baxter McKenzie! You've no right to read someone else's personal—"

"My arm's sore!" he croaked.

"If it wasn't, it'd definitely be sore now!" She laughed, and lay down thinking, So what, I'll probably never write in that diary again. If she did, Baxie could read as much as he wanted. He could do anything, as long as he got better. She tried to remember the noise of the plane's engine. Did it go in a straight line? Or in a circle?

Robbie said, "By now, Aunt Allie's in Las Vegas with her boyfriend. Isn't Las Vegas the place where people get married?"

She shrugged in the dark. "I don't know."

Robbie said, "Miss Alison Hunter marries Mr. John—what's his other name?"

"Macaroni," said Baxter. "Amore, baby."

They laughed not because it was all that funny, but because Baxter, in spite of his sore arm, was back to some of his old smart-lip talk.

Robbie said, "Could be she didn't even get to America. She wasn't leaving until eight o'clock at night. Mum and Dad probably called her on her cell phone. The news could have been on TV at Auckland Airport."

There was no laughter after that, and not much talking. They lay on the hard earth, listening to the sound of the stream, and it seemed that the whole of the earth was drowning.

When Jordan opened her eyes, she felt that she was looking through the kaleidoscope at shapes dancing on the wall of the cave. It was a few seconds before she realised she was seeing reflections of sunlight filtered through leaves moving in a salt breeze. She sat, buoyant with the first good feelings she'd had in this place. "Robbie! Baxter! We can make a fire!"

Drops of water still fell over the entrance, but now they were crystals of light and the tree fern was shining, its new fronds sleek with brown hair, its leaves a drying umbrella.

"A Christmas tree!" said Jordan. Of course it didn't look anything like a Christmas tree, but that was the description that matched her feeling. Yes, it was another hunch, a good one. "Robbie? Baxter? This is the day!"

There was work to be done. Baxter's arm was the right size but still red and sore. She needed to draw the wound yet again and put on another poultice. But the most important thing was fire. If they could light a fire on the beach and send smoke high into the clear air, then tonight, surely tonight, they would be back in Invercargill in their own beds.

"Cooked fish!" said Baxter. "Real food!"

Robbie cut the mound of glass from the end of Baxter's kaleidoscope and Jordan scrunched the purple tissue paper that had been wrapped around the presents. There was a lot of firewood around, all of it wet, but Jordan told Robbie how to use the pocket knife to peel away the wet outer layer and then shave off dry strips.

"How do you know that?" he asked.

"Just do it!" she said.

Robbie gave a theatrical sigh. "Voices in your head." But he, too, was in a good mood. The sunlight bouncing off their skin also danced inside them, Jordan thought.

They decided that the fire should be above the beach so that the full tide would not put it out. Because the grass was long and wet, they had to clear a patch and put stones over it.

In the sun, the sound looked very different. The mountains were sharp against the sky, layers of navy blue and grey with snow-creased tops, and the bush glinted sparks of wetness. As for the sea, it was no longer dark, but a sheet of silver rippled with a light, warm wind. That breeze meant no sand flies, which just about made the morning perfect.

Jordan reflected that until this morning, everything they'd done had involved struggle and a certain amount

142

of failure. The fire, though, was Swiss Family Robinson stuff, too easy to be true. The sun cast a small image of itself through the kaleidoscope glass onto the purple tissue paper. They watched as the bright yellow disc darkened to brown, smoked, and curled the paper away from a hole. The first flames were almost invisible in the bright light, but they spread quickly. Fire embraced the bunch of crushed tissue and may have gone out without igniting the wood shavings except that they were ready with the pyramid book. Robbie yanked out the pages one by one and Jordan fed them to the flames. The wood shavings blackened at the edges. They put more on, shavings, paper, then bigger sticks with the wet bark peeled off. It wasn't long before they had a real fire that scorched the stones, devouring everything they fed it. They stacked wet branches beside it, turning them so that they would dry, and they saw how a little wetness in the wood thickened the smoke that climbed in a waving plume far above the tree line.

The other bright thing in the bay was Jordan's shirt tied with flax to the main branch of the broken tree. It was stirring in the wind, as a flag should. When Jordan looked at it, she felt uncomfortable and wished that it had been some colour other than red—yellow, perhaps, or white.

It could stay there. She would never wear it.

The rest of the wet clothes was draped over grass and branches, and a light steam was coming off them.

Baxter didn't want to sit in the cave on his own. Jordan held his good arm and helped him out, slowly through the trees, through the grasses. He sat by the fire and scratched at old sand-fly bites. Robbie got him some flax jelly to soothe the itch. "No sand flies today," he said. "It's the wind. It blows their wings off course."

"Like us," said Baxter. The redness had gone from his face. He was pale except for half a dozen sand-fly lumps on his forehead and one below his left eye. He put his hand on his stomach. "I'm hungry."

"We all are," said Jordan. "We'll get some fish."

Baxie squinted through smoke. "Cooked?"

"You bet."

The breeze blew the smoke around and several times they had to scramble away from the fire, coughing and blinking. The flames crackled and roared, the sun shone, and after days of feeling cold, they found themselves moving into shade to avoid the heat.

"A seal!" cried Robbie, pointing.

Something the size of a coconut bobbed out in the bay. It could have been anything, but then a dark, shining body appeared. It turned and put a flipper in the air.

"There used to be thousands of seals in these sounds," Jordan said. "Thousands and thousands. They were slaughtered to make fur coats for wealthy people in Europe."

The seal seemed to be waving to them. Then it dived, leaving rings of ripples on the silver water.

"I'm really very hungry," Baxter said.

Jordan threw some wood into the flames. "Do you

think you can look after the fire for us while we catch fish?"

Robbie spread their flax fishing line out on the beach. A couple of strands were coming undone, but the most important thing was to replace the safety-pin hook that had snapped when they landed yesterday's cod. Jordan was tying in the new pin when the air shook with a great shuddering roar.

There was no warning. The helicopter brought its noise with it. Suddenly, it appeared around the headland, halfway between the mountaintops and the water, a red-and-white dragonfly churning the morning air.

They jumped up, yelling and waving, and ran to the edge of the grass, where the water lapped over their bare feet.

"Here!" Robbie shouted. "Over here."

They all yelled at the chopper, even though they knew they couldn't be heard. Baxter's good arm was trembling with effort.

"Yes, yes!" Jordan crossed her hands at her throat. "They've seen us! They're coming over!" She breathed the words softly. "Haere mai! Haere mai!"

The red-and-white dragonfly swelled into a flying machine with a huge glass eye. It swept over the sound, ruffling the water and shaking trees. Directly toward the fire it came, over their heads as they waved, over the trees and on up the valley.

"They saw us!" Robbie cried.

"But there's nowhere to land," Jordan said, and she felt like crying.

"On the grass!" said Baxter. "They can land on the grass!"

"Not big enough," said Robbie. "Those trees. The rotors could get—" He stopped and Jordan knew that he was thinking about Harold again.

She listened. The engine noise throbbed to a thinness and then, oh, yes, it increased! The chopper was coming back, lower this time, approaching with a roar that squinted their eyes and put their hands over their ears. Over the trees it stormed, sending branches into spasms, scattering fire smoke and ashes. Through the rushing wind something fluttered down, turning end over end to land in the bushes behind them.

A few seconds later the helicopter was flying up the sound, shrinking once more to dragonfly size.

Jordan was first to get to the yellow object that had been caught in the lower branches of a rimu tree. It was yellow paper held by a rubber band around a block of milk chocolate. On the paper in scrawly ballpoint were the words BACK SOON!

Now Jordan cried. She sat down on the grass and bawled out loud, tears running down her face and blurring the view of the sunlit bay. Robbie smiled and put his arm around her. She thought he was giving her a hug, and so he was, but only on the way to lifting the chocolate from her hand.

"Baxie?" he called. "Baxie? Guess what you've got for breakfast!"

CHAPTER TWENTY-FIVE

1 8 0 5

Hunter punched his chest in frustration. He who had such stealth he could lift a trout from a stream with his hands had betrayed himself with clumsiness, first the bush stripped of leaves and now falling rocks that revealed his hiding place to those who would kill him. Even now, they would be climbing the slope, hand over hand, their eyes sharp with the excitement of the chase. There could be no hesitation.

He had no weapons, but two things gave him hope. The warriors thought he was wounded and ill with fever. Also, there was still some mist on the slope that would hide him from their spears. He stayed as much as possible in the grey fog and sidestepped down the slope, less concerned now with noise than with speed. When he came out below the mist, he crouched, hoping that the scrub would provide him with cover. But someone saw him. He heard a shout and paused. Between him and the bay of the dying moon, there was an outcrop of rocks. On these stood a man waving a club as a signal to others.

Hunter sprang out from the cliff, arching his body over the stunted scrub. He heard another shout, saw the sea rushing up to meet his outstretched hands. Then there was the sound of water in his ears as his body slid into a sheath of coldness.

It was a good dive that had carried him well out from the shore, and he had plenty of air in his lungs. The wet sealskin on his feet hampered his swimming but gave him extra weight so that he was able to stay well under the water. They would be watching. They might even be swimming after him. He kept going straight out into the bay, hoping to get beyond spear range before his breath gave out. When he did come up for air, he rolled onto his back and allowed only his nose and mouth out of the water.

With so much rain, so many streams and waterfalls, the top layer of the sea tasted almost fresh. It was also much warmer than the salt layer beneath him, but he had to go deep again, lest he leave ripples on the surface. He kept going, his breath trickling out in silver bubbles, his feet slower, heavier. The intervals between breaths grew shorter. After the seventh or eighth surfacing, he allowed his head to come upright so that he could see the shore. At once, a clamour broke out along the beach, and a group of men swarmed about like shorebirds. They had seen him, but as far as he could make out, there was no one following him. He was more than halfway across the sound and for now, he was safe.

He didn't bother to go under again. He swam on the surface, their curses echoing behind him. He kept going, one arm over another, until he was within reach of the rocky shore, then he grabbed an overhanging tree and pulled himself out of the water.

On the other side, the men were now as big as flies, much smaller than the curses that still echoed across the water. The chase was over today, but it would soon resume. They would not stop until they caught him.

Crossing the water had increased the distance to the huhu camp by several days. He would now have to travel to the head of the sound and back up the other side to cross the mountains. How much simpler it would have been if he had kept running after he'd seen Toru.

He squeezed the water from his hair and closed his eyes, saw in his moe-mahi a wood pigeon in a tree behind him. "Marama?" he said aloud, but she did not appear. He sighed, feeling both satisfaction and disappointment.

Marama no longer needed him.

She and her brothers were out of danger.

CHAPTER TWENTY-SIX

2 0 0 5

They didn't go fishing. Robbie stayed with Baxter by the fire while Jordan returned to the cave for their shoes and bags. As she entered the earth hollow, she looked around her at the walls freckled with light and was almost sorry to be leaving it. Yesterday she hated this cave. Today it was the hand of Papatuanuku, the earth mother, who had been holding them safe and dry through an experience that had been a terrible storm. Jordan leaned sideways to put her cheek against a wall. She would not have been surprised to feel it warm, to hear a beating heart amongst all those tree roots, as she breathed in the smell of clay and felt the earth, fine as biscuit crumbs, against her skin. It wasn't a big cave, but it had been good to them, and if it was haunted, it was by a good ghost. For that matter, there were probably ghosts everywhere, people, animals, birds, all leaving little bundles of energy in the air. Did plants have ghosts? She wasn't sure. All she did know was that someone or something had been calling her by her Maori name and telling her things she needed to know. The voice wasn't there now, but then, now she didn't need it. Perhaps, she thought, that's what guardian angels really were—ghosts, your family and friends who'd passed on, hanging around to look after you.

• • •

Robbie wanted to take the fishing line as a souvenir. They curled it into the cake tin and put it in the bag with the wet clothes. Everything packed, they sat a little way from the fire, waiting for the return of the helicopter, imagining it in the sunlight on the other side of the sound. "They'll have rescue equipment," Robbie explained to Baxie. "It'll hover and someone'll come down. You know, on a ladder, like sea rescues."

Baxter's smile was ringed with chocolate. "A spider on a string."

It was amazing, thought Jordan, what a sugar fix could do for Baxter. "They'll take us up one at a time," she told him. "You can go first."

After days of dark rain, the sea was now shimmering as though it were drawing the sun in to feed itself. Rags of mist moved up the mountain slopes and waterfalls fell in white ribbons down rock faces. Everything shone with light.

There was a plop of water near the shore. The seal had come back to look at them, and this time it had a mate. Two dark heads bobbed in the glistening sea, and from this distance they looked like a couple of Labrador dogs.

"It was a terrible thing," said Jordan, "the way New Zealand's first English settlers killed seals by the thousands. It was worse, even, than the whaling."

"Mum's great-grandfather was one of those," said Baxter.

"No, he wasn't," said Robbie.

"Not her great-grandfather," said Jordan. "He was her great-great-great—oh, I don't know—about six greats. He wasn't English. He was Maori and he didn't hunt seals. He just lived with sealers before he came to Invercargill."

"He had an English name," Robbie said.

"People called him Charlie Hunter, but that wasn't his real name. He was definitely Maori." Jordan put another branch on the fire. It hissed and thick white steam mixed with the smoke. Charlie Hunter was the reason why her geneology project wasn't finished. He was a blind alley. She didn't even know his iwi—his tribe.

"Hunter used to be Mum's real name," said Baxter, "and Aunt Allie's real name and Grandad's real name."

"I am absolutely positive," said Jordan, "that he didn't kill seals for the fur trade." Actually, she was positive about nothing except the need to be positive. All she knew about Charlie Hunter was that he'd lived with some English sealers until 1808, when he'd married a Scottish woman. They'd had six sons and five daughters.

"Jordan?" Robbie touched her hand.

"What?"

"Do you want your red shirt?"

"No!" she said too loudly, too quickly, and there was a silence. Someone would pull up the Cessna, she told herself. Harold would have a real funeral.

Out of habit, she looked at her watch. It was useless, its face swimming with water. She couldn't believe that just last week they were shopping in Wellington and she had spent all her pocket money on the most beautiful scarf she'd ever seen. In less than a week, that rainbow scarf had aged a hundred years, and so had she.

The fire died down to a bed of grey embers while they watched the hills for the red-and-white dragonfly, but it wasn't the helicopter that came into the bay. It was an orange twin-hulled boat motoring around the headland so fast that two wings of spray flew out behind it.

Jordan caught her breath. Waka, she thought. Toia mai, he waka! Haul in the canoe! Then she breathed out in a gust of laughter. Stink! If it didn't throttle back, it'd run right up the beach and into their fire.

Robbie was already standing at the water's edge, a bag in each hand, as though he were waiting at a bus stop.

Jordan helped Baxter to his feet. She grabbed a handful of grass and tried to wipe some of the chocolate from his mouth. "It's okay, Baxie," she said. "We're going home."

A Note from the Author

IT IS ALMOST IMPOSSIBLE TO WRITE MAORI HISTORICAL
fiction. Such is the structure of Maori society—*iwi* (tribe),
hapu (sub-tribe) and *whanau* (family)—that as soon as a
name is mentioned, a character can be historically placed
in some part of Aotearoa New Zealand. Because this story
was important to me, and because it could only be told in
fiction, I have blurred names. No tribe is identified and the
characters have been named to match their personality or
position instead of having a true family name. Anything
that could suggest a specific location has also been
blurred. But in a nonspecific way, I have tried to remain
true to Maori culture and the spirituality of the land.

No one knows when the last moa died, but there is
some evidence that this great bird survived in the South
Island until the early nineteenth century. About this time
there were also English seal hunters in a sound in Fiordland, a remote southwest area of the South Island, now a
national park. It is said that these sealers had some
association with a runaway slave who lived in a cave in
Doubtful Sound.

These were some of the factual seeds that grew into the
work of fiction.

Joy Cowley